AF447482

2026 First Edition

Published in the United States by March Lee Ang.

Paperback ISBN 979-8-234-05800-3

Printed in the United States of America on acid-free paper

www.2084novel.com

Book design by March Lee Ang

2084

March Lee Ang

"The Party told you to reject the evidence of your eyes and ears. It was their final, most essential command."

George Orwell

1984

1

It was a sweltering February day in Washington DC. The sky was a hazy grey blue, like dried concrete, and the sun was a relentless spotlight on anyone caught in her gaze. Marshall Smith was anxious to get home but walked at his normal pace, staying in the shadows of the buildings as much as he could to avoid the direct sunlight. Slim-built and quiet, Marshall was a thirty-eight-year-old rule-following citizen who, much like everyone else, feared the consequences of stepping over any line that may expose him as anything less than an absolute patriot. He had never done anything remotely treasonous in his entire life until a few months ago.

When Marshall reached his place, he looked up at the dirty red brick, four story apartment building in Prospera Haven. Approximately five decades ago, his building, along with every other identical building in the neighborhood, was constructed by Frederick Building Corp after the area, formally known as Anacostia, was bulldozed and the less desirable residents moved out in the name of development, strengthening of the country, and cleaning up of the nation's capital. Like every other building on the block, it had eight windows per story (aside from the first floor, which had six and an entrance door in the middle), contained sixteen apartments, and wore upon its facade decades of sad neglect.

The walk from the bus stop to his home was only a short ten minutes, but in that time the combination of heat and anxiety had already caused Marshall to sweat through his undershirt; his white dress shirt was starting to splotch; and his light tan khaki pants were sticking uncomfortably to his legs.

His phone vibrated in his pocket just as he was about to reach for the front door handle. Instinctively, he reached into his pocket and pulled it out. It was a Facts Social update. Four Resistance terrorists had just been apprehended in Chicago in a failed attempt to blow up a local hospital. The president would address the nation later that evening.

Marshall put the phone back in his pocket and opened the front door, hoping for a rush of cool, air-conditioned relief. Instead, he walked into a wall of soupy hot lobby air.

God damn AC's still out, Marshall thought sadly to himself and wondered why he was still hopeful that it would have been fixed.

Mrs. Johnson, an older woman of about sixty in a threadbare blue flower dress, short black pumps, and too much makeup stood by the row of brass mailboxes checking for letters. The box, as all mailboxes have been for decades, was empty. Above the bank of boxes was the same gold framed photograph of the Holy American President that donned the entrance of every apartment, business, and government building in the country. The portrait was that of a square faced man of between fifty and seventy, with blond hair combed to his left, bluish brown eyes, and a stern face that read "do not cross me." He wore a dark blue suit, a red tie, and his right hand pointed forward, as if out of the photo and directly at the viewer.

Upon hearing Marshall enter, Mrs. Johnson turned and her mind seemed to snap back to the present, as her disappointed face quickly shifted into an emotionless smile.

"Good afternoon, Mr. Smith," she greeted him with a cheerful voice that did not reach her eyes.

Marshall smiled back. "Good afternoon, Mrs. Johnson," he replied. Marshall saw Mrs. Johnson at least a few times a week by this mailbox, part of her mind several decades in the past, waiting for a letter that would not come from a daughter who had been erased. "A hot one today. I hear it might hit a hundred and ten tomorrow. Hope they get the air fixed by then."

"I'm sure they will, dear. The boys at Frederick Management are the best. They'll have it fixed in no time!" She said with a less than optimistic tone as she glanced nervously at Marshall's pants pocket.

"You're right, of course," Marshall replied and began walking directly towards the stairs. The elevator had been out of order for some time now and he stopped bothering to check it months ago. "Have a nice night now."

"You too, dear" Mrs. Johnson said as she turned back towards her first-floor apartment.

Marshall had the urge to run up the stairs two at a time, but he knew that would sound suspicious, and he did not want to get his heart racing. So he walked up one step at a time as he normally did. He finally got to his third-floor apartment door and looked into the retinal scanner in the middle of the door. The door slid open, Marshall took a step through, and the door quickly slid back shut.

The apartment was a small, one bedroom, one bathroom unit. He walked into the main living space, which was sparsely furnished with a table for two–which had never sat more than one–a couch barely large enough for three facing a wall mounted television screen, and a faux-wood coffee table. His only picture screen was hung above the couch and currently showed an image of a mountain range in the springtime. The apartment was stifling. He opened the window by the couch, placed a box fan that was sitting on the floor in the windowsill facing out so as not to blow the sunbaked hot air into the apartment, and turned it to high. He then went into his bedroom, walked around his twin sized bed, opened the window, and placed a fan there too.

Perhaps it's good that the AC is out. The fan noise might give me some cover.

Marshall then carefully went through his normal routine. He placed his phone on the bedside table and began slowly stripping off his sweat soaked clothing. When he took off his pants, he was careful not to let the object in his left pocket hit the floor and make any noise. He then brought the day's clothes into the bathroom, placed them in the washing machine, and turned on the shower. *I wish I normally closed the bathroom door to shower*, he thought. But he normally did not so he left it open. He turned back to the washing machine and quietly removed the box from his pants pocket, carefully unlocked it, opened the lid, and looked down at the old smartphone nestled within.

2

Marshall was given the phone in an antique store, which he had stumbled into after work one Tuesday afternoon two months back. The exterior of the store was inconsequential in every way. It had dusty storefront windows that were difficult to see through, with peeling, faded old English gold lettering, which had once spelled out "Blair's Antiques." Marshall had passed by this store hundreds of times as he walked home from the bus stop down Thurmond Avenue and not once noticed its existence. At the very moment he was passing Blair's Antiques that fateful afternoon, he saw Michael Black Cain about a hundred yards ahead walking towards him talking to another man he did not recognize. Desperate to avoid another lengthy conversation about heretics, Marshall quickly ducked into the first door he saw, which happened to be Blair's Antiques.

The dusty wood framed glass door opened easily, and a small brass bell jingled cheerfully in response. He walked into a musty smelling, weakly air-conditioned room filled with old wooden furniture, lamps, bookcases (which were generally worthless since the Great Digitization), and random tchotchkes. The store was dimly illuminated by a soft yellow light, which Marshall immediately found soothing compared to the harsh white light in most of the buildings he entered these days.

"Good afternoon!" came a friendly, distinctly older, voice from Marshall's left.

Marshall glanced over to find a kindly looking man of at least sixty-five sporting an old-fashioned light brown tweed jacket and a dark brown tie standing behind a long counter. He had the air of an old tree, aged and sturdy, and filled with quiet knowledge. The Holy American President pointed at Marshall from the portrait hanging on the wall behind the counter.

"Hello," Marshall responded, half looking at the man, half peering out of the window to see if Michael had spotted him.

"I don't get many customers these days. Is there anything in particular I could help you find?" he asked, hopefully.

"Oh, um, no, nothing in particular. I'm just...looking." At that moment Marshall saw Michael approaching. He quickly took several steps into the store and turned a corner past a tall bookcase that was filled with faded porcelain nativity figurines.

The shopkeeper walked into the aisle. "Hiding from someone?" he asked amusedly. Marshall took a breath and looked over at the man. "Eric," the man said, offering his hand. Marshall peered at the man suspiciously for half a heartbeat. The shopkeeper had a long and angular face, slightly wrinkled from time, a sharp nose and a slim moustache, topped with dark brown hair, parted to the left side. Despite the acute angles of his face, the overall impression it gave was a friendly one. Marshall extended his hand.

"Marshall," he replied as their hands shook.

"Well, while you're hiding you might as well take a peek around. I have some fun pieces here and there. Desks and furniture to be sure, but also little knickknacks from forgotten times."

Marshall took a few steps further into the shop, his eyes scanning the dusty items in the room: a jar of little green plastic soldiers, an old set of cutleries, a series of glass paperweights, a green painted tin watering can. There was a ship in a bottle with one mast broken tucked away behind a series of mugs in the shapes of different animal heads. Things that Marshall would never need, nor have the extra money for, in the first place.

He then saw a watch in a small glass case on a desk to his left. It was gold and analog, which was exceedingly rare to find as analog watch production was halted at least thirty years back. The watch reminded Marshall of one from the past, but he could not place it.

"Ah, that's a beauty. It's from the last century, you know."

"How much?"

"Two," Eric replied hopefully.

Marshall opened the case and picked up the watch. He wound the crown and the watch began to tick.

"See? Still works," Eric nodded his head.

Two thousand dollars was more than Marshall could spend on something superfluous. He only made twenty-five thousand a month and barely had enough to cover his apartment, food, and other essentials. He'd been using the same razor for months. Eric sensed his hesitation.

"How about you take it, try it on for a week. Come back and if you like it, we can talk about price. I can trust you to come back, right?"

Marshall slipped the watch on. The cool metal felt at home on his wrist. He put his arm down and felt the weight of it. He noticed the watch did not slip up or down as he moved. A perfect fit. "Okay," Marshall said. "I'll try it on and come back next week."

Eric smiled at him. "It's a deal."

As Marshall stepped out of the store, he sensed that the old shopkeeper was more pleased that he'd be coming back in a week than at the potential sale of the watch.

* * *

Most of Marshall's weeks were the same as every other. He worked Monday through Saturday and had Services on Sunday, which everyone was required to attend. Marshall worked at the Agency of Historical Accuracy, housed on the fourth and fifth floors of the Department of Cultural Freedom building. Located at the corner of 14th street South West and Independence Avenue, the imposing stone-gray building with Corinthian columns faced the National Mall and was across 14th street from the Christopher Columbus museum.

Each morning, Marshall arrived at 7:35 in the morning to get into the queue of men who looked like they were attending a dress-coded family reunion. A sea of dark blond to light brown to dark brown hair, on top of brown or blue eyes set in ivory-toned faces, thin sharp noses, and cleanly shaved chins. Each man wore a white button up shirt tucked into black or dark blue or brown slacks above black or brown shoes—the department's allowance for fashionable creativity. Personal watches were definitely not allowed. Once he neared the front of the line, Marshall lifted up his chin and creased his mouth into the same half smile that everyone else wore, that of a man who was satisfied with his work and loved his country. It took at least fifteen minutes to get through the metal detectors, x-ray machines, security pat downs, retinal and palm scans, and voice ID check before he was able to enter. The building was well air conditioned, and Marshall was grateful for that each day he walked in, as it was generally already sweltering by seven in the morning during the winter months, and almost unbearable outside during the summer months.

The Friday morning after Marshall's accidental stumble into Blair's Antiques was no different than any other. Upon entering the building, Marshall walked into the grand entrance hall with vast ceilings held up by massive stone columns that encircled the area and appeared to be leaning in when one looked at them long enough. Straight ahead was a three-story tall picture of the Holy American President, eyes gleaming with purpose, his finger tip the size of a small car pointing directly at him as he walked in.

Marshall walked over to the right and joined the throng of neatly dressed men at the bank of gold painted elevators. He kept his face staring ahead, hoping to avoid eye contact or conversation. Sometimes, Marshall had the energy to engage with his fellow workers but today was not one of those days. It took all of his focus and energy just to maintain a cheerful enough facade.

Marshall's phone vibrated in his pocket. He took the phone out to look at the notification. Another update of Facts. Just as he was about to read it, a hand landed on his shoulder.

"Marshall!" Marshall recognized the tinny voice of Michael Black Cain. Marshall took a short but deep breath, as if to gather strength directly from the air around him.

"Good morning, Michael." Marshall said with the cheerful voice that he had honed over the years and belonged solely in this particular building. He turned slightly to his left as Michael scooted past two white shirted men and drew up beside him.

Michael's physique was the embodiment of average: average height, average build, brown hair, and a triangular chin that came to a sharp point. He always had an enthusiastic yet somewhat suspicious look about him that reminded Marshall of a squirrel who had just found an unexpected store of nuts. Michael worked on the third floor at the Agency of Theology, and as such always spoke with the air of confidence that can only come from righteous superiority.

"Did you hear about the raid yesterday?" Michael asked. Every time Michael came up to him with news about some raid, immolation, or erasure, Marshall regretted sitting at his table during lunch on his first day nine years ago. He was bearable when talking about anything else, but his fervor for divine retribution always left Marshall feeling uneasy, especially because he had to eagerly agree with Michael's sentiments.

"I haven't. What happened?" Marshall said with as much genuine interest as he could muster.

"Just saw it on Facts a few seconds ago. Seventeen Muslims hiding out in Cheyenne. Can you believe it? I thought we were almost rid of them! Found them praying on those mats of theirs in a basement, like cockroaches. No doubt planning an attack right after. They were near Fort Warren. That was their most likely target, they said. It's terrifying! They could be anywhere!"

"How'd they know they were planning an attack?" Marshall asked, and quickly regretted asking a question that could be interpreted as skepticism of a story on Facts. But Michael did not seem to notice.

"Who knows. Didn't say. But the president's always right."

"The president's always right," Marshall repeated the mantra without thinking.

"Glad they got them though. Seventeen! I still can't believe it. Probably part of that cursed Resistance. Do you have any idea how much damage seventeen of those animals could do?"

"A lot."

"You're damn right, a lot. I don't understand how people can become like that. How lucky are they that they can live in this country? We give them a job in the mines, they get enough to eat and live, and this is how they repay us. I mean, who are they praying to anyway? Everyone knows their god," Michael made air quotations with his fingers, "doesn't exist. Made up by some heretic to mind control people, you know." Marshall had heard this speech before. "Suicide bombers, 72 virgins, they're animals! Can you believe there are still people so stupid they actually believe that garbage?"

"It's unbelievable," Marshall agreed.

"I wonder what they'll do with them. Erasure isn't enough in my opinion. Haven't had a public immolation in months. The president must show his strength. Send a message. We won't tolerate these heretics in our country. I'm going to tell Paul myself," Michael inserted inferences of his apparent closeness with the head of his agency, Paul Kane, as often as he could. "Seventeen! If there's seventeen in just one place, maybe there's more than we thought left. Have to teach these cockroaches a lesson!"

The gold painted elevator doors for the fifth floor, Marshall's floor, slid open to Marshall's relief.

"Glad they got those terrorists," Marshall agreed and then nodded his head towards the elevator door.

"Alright, well no doubt I have a busy day ahead of me with this so probably won't see you at lunch, but I'll see you at service on Sunday," Michael said, self-importantly.

"Yeah, I'll see you Sunday. Good luck with all that."

Fourteen men, including Marshall, herded themselves into the small rectangular box. Marshall recognized all of them but had never spoken to any of them and had no desire to on this particular morning. Fraternization within his agency was frowned upon anyway. Cameras in the elevator identified each person and allowed the elevator to move only if everyone inside was authorized for the fifth floor. The elevator sped quickly up, stopped, and the doors slid open on the fifth floor, where the men filed out into a long echoey hallway with bright fluorescent lights, dark maroon stone floors, grey polished walls, and thin, tasteless air. The hall was lined with dark wooden doors and small signs that indicated which office was behind each door. Straight ahead facing the elevator doors was a large sign that read The Agency of Historical Accuracy. This agency was one of the largest in the federal government, spread across the entire country; there were at least two offices in fifty-five of the fifty-nine states. Wyoming, Starland (formally Greenland), The North (formally Yukon, Nunavut, and the Northwest Territories), and Reeve Island (formally Prince Edward Island), all had one.

He had never been to any of the other floors, but he assumed they looked the same as this one. Marshall's door was the one at the end of the hall. Marshall hated the walk. His shoes always clicked against the stone floor, and he could hear the echo of his own steps reverberate back to him, as if he was following himself down the hallway. The other men filtered away through their own doors and Marshall made his way to his.

He turned the gold gilded doorknob and stepped into a large open room that covered almost the entire west wing of the building. He glanced over the rows of cubicles and made his way down the middle aisle, keeping his view straight ahead as it was illegal to even glance at a government workstation that was not one's own. He never knew how many people were working at any particular time, as this agency was active every single second of the day, with workers coming in shifts to cover every hour. Small half globe cameras popped out of the ceiling at every intersection. Miniaturized cameras could have been installed instead, which would have been practically invisible. The larger, visible cameras made it clear that they wanted people to be cognizant of the fact that they were being watched.

His cubicle was identical to every other cubicle. He had a chair and a large touch screen display attached to the back wall. A headset hung on the side that allowed him to give voice commands when necessary. A digital clock with red numbers showed the time next to the headset. No personal items were allowed, as he shared the cubicle with other Erasers.

As soon as Marshall sat down, the screen extended out to within arm's reach of his chair and turned on. He put the headset on and adjusted the microphone to his mouth.

"Marshall Smith, November twenty fifth, twenty eighty-three," he glanced at the clock. "Seven fifty-seven AM." The display turned on and showed a mosaic of photographs, each with the same man in it. He looked to be in his twenties or early thirties, with skin the color of lightly creamed coffee, and sporting a lanky frame. He was alone in most of the pictures and rarely was he smiling. In the top left corner of the screen was his Identity Card photograph, which Marshall could rotate completely around with his fingers. Below this photo read: Erased, 11/21/2083. *Good, an easy file,* Marshall thought. In fact, his first two files of the day were easy. All were men around the same age, mostly solo in their photographs, and each file only contained a few hundred photographs. Solo shots were the easiest as he just had to select them and whisper "delete." The more candid photos where the subject was interacting with others were trickier, as removing the subject often made the positions of the others in the picture nonsensical. Sometimes, he was able to use other photographs from the collection to swap the subject out. When there was a particular friend group that appeared multiple times, Marshall could find one of the friends that were missing from the photograph, most likely the one who took the photo, and replaced the subject with that person by selecting them in another photograph and dragging them into the photograph he was correcting. The computer adjusted the image of the friend to match the subject's body position.

When the erasures first started, the more people connected to the ones being erased, the more difficult the process. But as time went on, and those who complained and made a ruckus were erased themselves, the easier it became. Marshall was told his work was a gift to ease the pain of an erasure, and he even tried to believe it. Without any photographic or video evidence that the person ever existed, it was easier to doubt one's own memories of the person. Doubt eventually blossomed into denial, and at that point when a memory of an erased person ignited in one's head, an equally strong thought counteracted it: "what person?" That was the relief Marshall wanted to believe he gave to people. Not that they would ever know he was the one providing this relief. One whisper to anyone of what his job was, and Marshall knew he would be the next person to appear on one of these displays, erased from history. There were not any photographs of Marshall in anyone's photo library anyway.

He was going at a steady, mechanical pace and it was almost lunch time when her file showed up on the screen. Marshall was instantly drawn to her. She was tall with dark curly hair, bluish green eyes, a round face, and a wide Cheshire Cat smile. The photographs showed she mostly wore bohemian style clothing: diaphanous flower-patterned dresses and fashionably oversized knee-length coats, sun hats and ephemeral rompers. The loose-fitting clothes could not hide her obviously well-toned yet curvy figure. Marshall's breath caught in his throat and the brain fog of tedium lifted immediately as his mind snapped into focus. He quickly steadied his breathing. *She doesn't exist*, he thought to himself as he stared at a photograph of her standing at the edge of a terraced flower garden in a snug fitting royal blue dress that hit just below her knees. What struck Marshall most was not her beauty, but how he could sense a genuine happiness emanating from her in these photographs. That joy shook him. There was a sudden ball of hollowness right below his sternum. He continued to look longingly at the photograph, spiraling into a world of his own desire. It was not a romantic or sexual desire for this no-longer existing person, but a desire simply to be near her in the hopes that the joy she so clearly felt might somehow rub off onto him. The hope that maybe her proximity might cause him to smile the way she smiled. And there was something else. Something familiar, but he could not place it.

An image of the cameras above him abruptly thrust itself into his mind. Marshall shook his head and looked to the top left corner of the screen where her Identity Card photo was displayed. This was the one photo in which she was not smiling. Her lips were pursed and even her eyes seemed dulled. Below this picture in black lettering Marshall read: Erased, 11/24/2083.

I wonder what her name was, Marshall thought, instantly followed by the thought, *she never had a name*. A sigh attempted to escape his lungs, but Marshall's body instinctively stonewalled the air from liberation. He carefully began reviewing all the pictures of her pulled from the photo libraries of every person that knew her, scrolling and editing or deleting them as he went. In the images that still made sense without her, Marshall circled her with his fingers and whispered "erase," and the space was seamlessly filled in by the computer, so the image remained intact in her absence. He finished the file and looked up at the clock. It was long past two o'clock. He had missed lunch. Marshall's stomach grumbled, but there was nothing he could do about it. He opened the next file.

The rest of the day went by without incident, as Marshall switched his brain back to the machine-like task of accurizing the photo libraries of his fellow citizens. He felt some relief as the monotony of his work pushed the image of the beautiful woman with the joyful smile deep into the recesses of mind.

3

A week after Eric Blaire gave him the gold watch, Marshall walked back into the dusty antique shop. He had come directly after work and so did not have the gold watch on him. In fact, he had not worn the gold watch once since. He had decided to keep it the second he walked out of the antique shop with it on his wrist, one week ago. As soon as he had gotten home though, Marshall had carefully placed it in the drawer of his bedside nightstand and had left it there, unwilling to take it out. He knew he had not done anything illegal by buying this gold watch, yet something about it felt wrong and he always erred on the side of caution.

As soon as he stepped into the store, Marshall saw Eric Blaire sitting on a stool behind the counter, with a large smile on his face.

"I knew you'd be back!" Eric glanced down at Marshall's wrist to look for the watch.

"Not wearing it today. But don't worry, I'm going to keep it." Marshall stepped over to the counter and pulled out his phone, which instantly read his fingerprints on the case and lit up. Eric took out his phone in-kind. "Pay two thousand," Marshall commanded his phone as he tapped it to Eric's. The phone chimed and Marshall placed it back into his pocket.

"Thank you," Marshall said, as he began making his way back towards the door.

"Would you care for some coffee?" Eric asked, hopefully.

Marshall paused. His instinct was to leave the shop immediately. Entering the shop last week was odd enough, but staying for coffee was downright unnatural. Anything outside of one's predictable behavior could easily be red flagged by Skeyelink. But something in Marshall's gut yearned to stay. In an instant Marshall saw a crossroads. Outside the dusty glass of the shop's front door, he saw the concrete sidewalk and the blistering heat of the afternoon sun. He saw the walk home back to his lonely one-bedroom apartment on the third floor of the brick building with the broken elevator. He saw the sixty hours a week he spent at his terminal erasing other people's memories. That was the path he saw outside that door. And standing behind him was an old man offering him a cup of coffee. Somehow Marshall knew that that cup of coffee was an entirely different path.

The image of the woman with the dark curly hair suddenly sauntered into his mind's eye. Her beautifully joyful face filled his thoughts, smiled at him, and nodded. Somehow Marshall knew that this woman who no longer existed, whom he never met, and whose name he would never know, wanted him to have that cup of coffee. Somehow Marshall knew and with a deep breath he turned around.

"Sure, just one cup."

Eric's smile widened. "Just this way, I have a small kitchen in the back."

They

their way through a short maze of bookshelves filled with useless echoes of the memories of strangers, to a wooden door in the back. Marshall looked curiously at the door and noticed there were no biometric sensors, no keypad, and no place to touch one's phone. He wondered how the door was unlocked. Eric took out a small silver key, slipped it into the doorknob and turned it. To Marshall's surprise, the doorknob turned and the door pushed open.

"Why don't you use a phone reader or retinal scanner on the door?" Marshall asked. It was generally accepted that this was the most secure locking combination.

"Oh, I simply like the feel of a key in my hand," Eric replied with a wink as he flicked on a light switch on the wall.

Behind the door was a small kitchenette. A wooden table and two chairs stood against the left wall, and a counter ran the length of the wall on the right with a sink and an old coffee pot sitting on it. Against the back wall stood a short refrigerator next to another door, which Marshall noticed was also bare of any modern locking mechanisms. Eric walked over to the coffee pot, filled it with water from the sink, and began brewing some coffee. He then turned to Marshall.

"Please, have a seat," he gestured toward the table and chairs. "The coffee will take a few minutes"

Marshall sat down, not knowing what to do next. He asked the first question that came to mind: "How come you have so many bookshelves in your store?"

"My father owned a used bookstore in Boston. Growing up I spent most of my childhood in that store, when I wasn't in school, that is. We had few customers but the ones we did have were dedicated and came in often. Not that my father opened the store for the money. It was more a hobby to occupy him during his retirement. He loved to read and we spent many of our days in these large matching armchairs by the front windows reading with Marlowe, our tabby cat, purring in his lap. When he died, he passed it along to me. This was before the Great Digitization, of course. When the books were burned and the store closed, I couldn't bear to get rid of the bookcases. My father had built most of them himself, you know. So now they're here, collecting dust. They're good for holding all these little knickknacks I've collected throughout the years at least."

"Where'd you get all these things?" Marshall gestured with a head nod to the front of the store.

"Oh here and there. Actually, a lot of the things were my father's. I guess you could say he was a collector of nostalgia. We had a big Victorian home filled with things he had collected over the years. He loved going to yard sales and estate sales and buying up all kinds of junk. When he died, I moved back into the house and took over the store, until the Great Digitization that is. When that happened, I shut down the bookstore, sold the house, brought everything down here, and opened this shop. Been here ever since. How about you?"

Marshall felt a sudden knot in his stomach.

"I'm from here, DC."

"And your parents?"

"I, uh, I don't remember my parents. I mean, they died when I was very young. They died...um...in...in a car crash." Marshall lied. "Grew up in a PCRF."

"I see. That sounds...very hard."

"It wasn't. The President took care of us all." Marshall lied again.

"Of course," Eric said softly with an edge of pity in his voice.

The coffee finished brewing. The smell was strong and bold and filled the room with a rich, earthy smell of some long-forgotten memory. It was nothing like the watered-down powdered coffee Marshall was used to. Marshall felt relieved as Eric turned away from him and from the conversation to pull out two mugs from the cabinet below the counter. He poured coffee into both. "Cream or sugar?" he asked.

"No, thank you," Marshall replied. "Black is fine."

Eric handed him his mug and sat in the chair across from him, holding his own black coffee. Marshall felt the warm mug against his palms and relished the smell emanating from its contents, subconsciously prolonging the moment as his mind reached unsuccessfully for the echo of the past that the aroma was attempting to draw out. He glanced up and saw Eric peering at him over the top of his mug, observing him. He took a sip and savored the deep, toasty bitterness.

"Good, isn't it?" Eric asked with a slight smile on his face.

"Good? This is the best coffee I've ever had! This must have cost you a fortune!"

"There are few things I indulge in. One has to find the things that bring them joy in this world we live in and make sure to partake in them when we can, otherwise what's the point?"

"Sure, of course," Marshall agreed with him instantly, but quickly regretted his immediate response when Eric asked him:

"What kinds of things bring you joy, Marshall? What are the things you indulge in?"

Marshall took a long sip of coffee, trying to buy time while he searched his mind for an answer that was not there.

"I enjoy, um, I'm not sure. I don't know how to answer that." He took another sip of coffee.

"That's okay. That's not unusual these days. Maybe I can share this joy with you? You like the coffee?" Marshall nodded. "Why don't we make this a weekly thing? Lord knows I don't have much going on these days and the company would be nice."

Under normal circumstances, Marshall would have felt extreme suspicion at this moment. No one ever invited him to do anything that was not mandated by the Holy American President. All of this would have felt like a trap, setting him up so he could be turned in for treason. Not that he had done anything explicitly illegal. But the line between acts considered illegal and acts that one could be erased for was a canyon of ambiguity and subjectivity, and something about him, an Eraser for the Holy American President, sitting down with a non-government employee over a cup of pricelessly delicious coffee felt inherently illicit.

Yet for some reason Marshall felt an authenticity in this man that he did not normally encounter. There was a genuine kindness in his face that made it impossible for him to believe Eric would turn him in for anything. And he felt the same draw that he felt when Eric first asked him if he wanted a cup of coffee. Marshall was not exactly sure what this draw was. Perhaps it was the desire for some human connection–Eric had thrown a rope down into the well of loneliness in which Marshall resided. Perhaps it was a desire for some miniscule attempt at self-determination–Marshall never did anything that was not completely expected, or at least what he thought was expected of him. And perhaps it was the thrill of rebellion. In fact, it was a combination of all three, but at that moment, Marshall could not quite put his finger on any one of them. The one thing he did know with certainty, was the woman with the dark curly hair would want him to say yes.

"Yes, I'd like that."

"Good! I have a feeling this will be the start of something!"

"Something? What something?"

"We'll just have to find out together now won't we?" Eric winked at Marshall and for the first time in many years, Marshall mouth creased into a genuine smile. Not the breath-holding, resigned smile that he had perfected over the years at the Agency of Historical

Accuracy; or the contorted, tight-lipped smile he wore at Sunday services; but the relieved smile of one invited in from an exile he was not even aware of.

* * *

The next seven Tuesdays, Marshall had coffee with Eric in the room behind Blair's Antiques. At first, Eric did most of the talking. While Marshall felt an inherent and inexplicable trust in Eric, he did not feel completely comfortable speaking his mind. Not only was he weary of saying the wrong thing, knowing Skeyelink was in his pocket, he genuinely did not know what to say. Marshall's conversational abilities had atrophied, if they existed at all, having not had the opportunity for a genuine conversation with another human in as long as he could recall.

Eric, on the other hand, seemed completely at ease and eager to talk. He spoke without fear or apprehension about his own life, his parents, his schooling, and trips he had taken around the country. Marshall, who had never gone farther than Baltimore, was fascinated by Eric's life and his descriptions of different places he had visited—all within the United States, of course, as travel outside the country was not permitted by the Holy American President, to keep the American citizens safe from the barbarous foreigners.

One Tuesday, Eric described a cross-country trip he had taken with his father. Eric often told stories about his childhood and his father. Every time, Marshall felt a pang of jealousy, having no memory of his own father.

"We drove from Boston to California. Took us a month to go there and back during the summer between sixth and seventh grade. We had just buried my mother and he felt like we both needed to get out of town. We went across the north of the country and came back by way of the south. It was a beautiful country back then. I remember driving through endless fields of corn and wheat, swaying in the cool breeze, in the Midwest. The west coast was my favorite part of the trip, especially in California. We took long hikes through the forests with these huge trees called Redwoods that made us feel insignificantly small. It was like being on a different planet. Or a forest moon," Eric winked at Marshall, but Marshall did not understand the reference. Eric went on. "I remember my father pulling over along this long stretch of highway that was surrounded by nothing but the open sky and the red rocks of the deserts. I think we were in New Mexico or Utah or somewhere around there. The air was thin and crisp. I remember my father shutting off the engine. We got out of the car and walked about fifty yards into the desert and he told me to listen carefully. The sound of absolute silence was breathtaking. Oh! And the Grand Canyon. Marshall, one day you have to visit the Grand Canyon. Of course it's different now. It's all different now. The Colorado River is barely a trickle these days. But the canyon itself would still be beautiful."

"How is it all different?" Marshall had asked.

"Well, the plains are basically dust now. The rain is no longer steady there and when it does come it's extremely destructive. The fields are no longer farmable. In California, most of the trees have been cut down. The deserts are so hot they're practically impassable. It's...a different country now," Eric said sadly.

Talking about the past in this way was unusual and generally frowned upon, since it was general knowledge that every aspect of American life had steadily improved since the Holy American President came to power. But Eric often spoke in a manner that on the surface appeared as though there were no topics that were off limits. However, it became clear over time that there were some things Eric would not talk about. For instance, it was clear to Marshall that the antique business was not a flourishing one, yet Eric appeared to have plenty of money. Marshall wondered where he got it from but did not dare ask. It was clear to Marshall that Eric would divulge what he wanted to divulge, and he did not want to risk prying or offending him in any way. The questions that Marshall did feel comfortable asking, mostly seeking more details regarding topics Eric brought up himself, Eric answered completely and without hesitation.

Only once did Eric mention a partner, whom Marshall assumed was his wife. He used the word once in a single sentence, in a long story, thrown in like a detail about a tree seen at the side of the road. Marshall almost asked him about her but quickly bit his tongue, waiting to see if Eric would bring her up again, but he never did. Over time, Marshall realized that the mentioning of his wife was a mistake, an error that Eric glossed over as quickly as possible. With that realization, it became clear to Marshall that even though Eric's conversation style seemed freewheeling in nature, he was apparently quite deliberate with what he was talking about, no doubt due to Skeyelink's omnipotent presence.

These Tuesday coffees with Eric quickly became the highlight of Marshall's week. They never lasted more than an hour, but as soon as he stepped back out onto the concrete sidewalk each week, he began looking forward to next Tuesday. It was as if the little antique store was a world unto itself, where Marshall could escape from the insidious fears and tribulations of his everyday life, which he had just begun to recognize were lurking behind every dark corner of his mind.

Two months after Marshall first stepped into Blair's Antiques, he walked into the back room of the shop. Eric began brewing the coffee and then pulled a rectangular device out of the cabinet below the coffee maker. It was thin, black, and about twice the size of Marshall's phone. Marshall went to sit down in his normal chair when Eric quickly made a hand motion with his palm up indicating he should remain standing. He then put his right index finger to his lips. Marshall remained quiet. Eric placed the device on the table and held his thumb to the top of it for a moment until it lit up with multiple buttons on the screen. Eric tapped a few of them and to Marshall's surprise he heard his own voice come out of the device. He almost gasped but Eric quickly shot him a glance that clearly meant "don't say a word!"

"Black coffee as usual?" Eric's voice asked out of the device.

"Please," Marshall's voice responded.

The sound of a liquid being poured into a mug came through, followed by the sound of a mug being placed on the wooden table.

"Have I told you about the time I went to that World Series game with my father?" Eric's voice continued.

Eric then quietly slipped his phone out of his pocket and placed it gently on his seat and then indicated to Marshall to do the same. Marshall followed suit as he listened to his own voice talk to Eric's voice.

Eric walked over to the door at the back of the room next to the refrigerator and opened it. He gestured Marshall towards the door. Marshall walked through it as quietly as he could. Eric followed behind and then gently closed the door. Behind the door was a short landing and then stairs leading down. Eric quickly walked down the stairs with Marshall in tow.

"What was that thing?" Marshall asked.

"The voice box? A clever little thing, isn't it? It was an old AI Conversation Trainer. They used to make them for immigrants to practice their English, back when it was legal for other languages to be spoken and people who didn't speak English were allowed into the country. They would have conversations with an AI voice, and it would train them to speak English. I reprogrammed it to listen and imitate voices."

"So that thing's been listening to us this whole time?" Eric grew nervous.

"Yes. Don't worry, it's totally off Skeyelink. It will take what it's learned about us and what we've talked about and create new conversations that will sound just like us. Skeyelink will listen to it and think we're still in that room."

Four flights down there was another door. Eric took out another key, slipped it into the lock, opened the door, and flipped on a light switch.

Lights flickered to life and Marshall's eyes grew wide. Inside was a square concrete room about twelve feet wide by twelve feet long. There were paintings and pictures hung on every inch of the wall. Real paintings, as opposed to the digital displays connected to Skeyelink that would only show President approved images.

"What are these?" Marshall asked, gasping.

"Oh, just some old art. I paint. That's another one of my joys. Most of these are mine."

Marshall stepped in front of a large painting with an ornate gold frame. It was a painting of a grassy area with a tree in the middle that was surrounded by saplings. A man and a woman lay under the tree, a red sash hung on the branch above them.

"You painted this?"

Eric nodded.

"Where'd you get the paint? The canvas?" Marshall asked, shocked at the blatant illegality of all this. Paint was exclusively sold to building and management companies for utilitarian purposes only. Ink, pencils, pens, paper, any sort of writing implement were outlawed after the Great Digitization. All art had been confiscated and assumed to have been destroyed. All writing was now typed into devices attached to Skeyelink. All art was created using programs on Skeyelink connected devices and one could only display their own art creations on the digital displays after it had been approved. A sudden fear overtook Marshall's awe. Fooling Skeyelink with a fake conversation was one thing, but just being in this room would certainly mean his erasure.

"I have to go. Let me go," he said in a panic, moving towards the door.

"It's too late for all that," Eric said calmly.

"You set me up! You should have told me before you brought me down here! You've killed me!"

"Have a seat," Eric gestured towards two armchairs in the middle of the room. "Catch your breath. You wouldn't be here if deep down, you didn't want to be."

"What do you mean? I don't want to be here. I don't want to..."

"SIT DOWN," Eric's voice transformed from the kindly conversational one Marshall was used to, to a tone owned by someone used to being obeyed. Marshall timidly sat down. "Good. Now take a deep breath," his voice shifted back to normal and he smiled at Marshall.

Marshall took a moment and closed his eyes. He suddenly saw himself standing outside his apartment building. Men in black masks and bullet-proof vests swarmed him, roughly wrapped his head in a black bag, picked him up, and threw him into the trunk of a black sedan.

"One of my favorite writers once wrote, 'Fear is the mind-killer.' Have you heard this before?" Eric asked.

"No, no I haven't," Marshall mumbled almost incoherently, trying to stem the tide of trepidation that was coursing through his veins.

"Of course not. His books were all purged decades ago. But it's true. Nothing paralyzes a mind like fear." Eric sat in the armchair next to Marshall. He put his hand on Marshall's shoulder and Marshall instantly felt some relief, as if Eric was drawing Marshall's fear out of his body using his fingers. Eric sat back in his chair. "Marshall, let me ask you something. Do you enjoy your job?"

The question snapped Marshall's attention back to the present.

"My job?" Marshall had never mentioned being an Eraser to Eric or anyone else. It was something that everyone knew about, but no one acknowledged existed. Having it brought up so candidly caught Marshall completely off guard. He did not know how to answer the question. "Do you know what I do?"

"Yes, Marshall. You're an Eraser, are you not?"

"How did you...how do you..."

"Know? Marshall, I know all about you."

"You're...you're part of Skeyelink aren't you? You're..."

"Don't be ridiculous, Marshall. I'm as far from Skeyelink or HALE as one can get. I'm a recruiter, you see."

"A recruiter? A recruiter for what?"

"For The Resistance."

"The...The Resistance?"

"Yes, Marshall, The Resistance."

"You're...you're supposed to be a myth! And terrorists! You're all terrorists!"

"Well, which one is it, Marshall? Are we a myth or are we terrorists? We can't be both."

"I...I...They said...He said" Marshall stammered. He had unknowingly stepped through the looking glass, fallen into a deep, rabbit hole and was frantically trying to search for an exit, or at least a handhold to grasp onto. Eric smiled his soft smile and placed his hand on Marshall's.

"They said. He said. The president says. Yes, he says a lot of things that are both illogical and hypocritical. Half the things he says are contradictory to things he said in the past. Hell, sometimes he says things that contradict things he said in the same sentence! The truth is, we're neither, Marshall. We're not terrorists. And I can assure you we are real."

"Why? Why did you show me this? Why are you telling me this? I'm dead because of you!"

"We're all going to die, Marshall. We're all dead already. It's just a matter of how we get there."

"Yes, but I didn't ask for this!"

"No, you didn't. And I apologize for that. We can't exactly advertise for new recruits and if people who want to join can find us, well then so could the President, and then we'd all be dead. No, this is the only way, Marshall. We meet people by chance and see if they're the type that would join."

"Join? I don't want to join!"

"You already have, Marshall. You just don't know it yet."

"What do you mean? I haven't joined anything! I want out!"

"It's too late for that, Marshall. You'd be surprised how many people in the Resistance had this exact same response. Fear is the mind-killer, Marshall. Let it pass through you so you can open your eyes. Now let me ask you again, do you enjoy your job?"

"My job? I...I've been doing it for so long. I...don't know. It, um, it's a job. It's a paycheck, you know? It pays the rent. How did you know I was an Eraser?"

"That is something I'll have to explain another time." Eric glanced behind Marshall at an old analog clock on the wall, another antique of the past. "We haven't much time before you should go home. I know you have a lot of questions, Marshall. I've just shoved a red pill in your mouth, but it's up to you to swallow it."

"Red pill? What the hell are you talking about?"

"The world you live in, the world created by the government, where the President is always right, where foreigners are bloodthirsty barbarians, where those that don't look like us or those who disagree with the president are all terrorists who hate this country: it doesn't exist. It's only real as long as we go along with it. The people that you help erase, they're not all radical, extremist, left-wing cockroaches that you've been told they are. And their families are not comforted by the loss of their pictures. You've been fed a lie your entire life. Now the question is, are you ready to open your eyes?"

"I can't...I don't...I'm..." Marshall could not think of what to say. He could not even think of what to think.

"That's not a question you have to answer now. Go home, get some rest. Eat your normal dinner. Get up in the morning. Go to work tomorrow like nothing happened. Go about your week like nothing happened. And come back next week."

"Next week? Come back for what?"

"Your orientation."

"Orientation? I don't want an orientation! I don't want any of this! You're going to get me erased!"

"You don't have to come back if you don't want to Marshall. I'm not threatening you and if you don't come back, nothing will happen to you. Not by us, anyway. We don't punish those who don't listen to us, who don't agree with us. We're not the President. Here, let me give you something." Eric walked over to a small cabinet against the back wall, opened the top drawer, and pulled something out that was about the size of his hand. He came back over to Marshall, who was still sitting in his chair trying to calm his palpitating heart. Eric handed Marshall a cream-colored wooden box with dark, slivered inlays crisscrossing the top, creating an intricate and somewhat chaotic pattern.

"What is this?" Marshall inspected it.

"Can you see the four lines that intersect the corners of the box?"

Marshall looked carefully and noticed amongst the seemingly random pattern that all four corners had an inlay hitting it at different angles.

"Find the one that points directly at the center of the box. Hold your thumb to it and pull the inlay out a bit."

Marshall did so and to his surprise, the inlay moved off the edge of the box about a quarter inch.

"Now go clockwise and do the same to each of the corners."

Marshall repeated the process three more times. After the last one, he felt something in the top of the box give way.

"Open the box, Marshall."

Inside was a thin black object, about six inches long by three inches wide. He looked up at Eric, confusion on his face.

"It's a phone, Marshall. A very old phone. About fifty years old, in fact. It was shut down right before Skeyelink fully took over. Everything in it that could connect it to Skeyelink has been shut down, so no one will be seeing what you do with it."

"Does it...does it work?"

"Of course it works! It's one of the first to use the nuclear batteries that are in our phones now, so it will still work for decades to come."

Marshall turned the antique phone over. It was much thicker and heavier than his current phone, which was barely thicker than a piece of cardboard.

"I shouldn't have this. You shouldn't have this!"

"And yet we do. Take it, it's yours. Keep it safe and hidden."

"What am I supposed to do with this?"

"Whatever you like. I'm sure you'll figure out what to do. There's only one rule. Don't use any names. Don't write any specifics. Don't put anything in here that you wouldn't want them to see. Just in case." He gently grabbed the phone, placed it back in the box, replaced the lid, and pushed the corner inlays back into place one at a time, locking it shut. He handed the box back to Marshall.

"Names? Write? I don't understand."

"It's time to go now. I'll see you next week."

Marshall placed the box into his pants pocket. "Why do you think I'll be back next week?" Marshall asked accusatorially.

Eric smiled a knowing smile. "Come, it's time to go."

He led Marshall back upstairs and into the small kitchen behind the store where the voice box was still imitating their conversation. Eric pressed a button on the device and Marshall heard his own voice say, "Well, I have to get going. Same time next week?" The box made the sound of a coffee mug being placed on the table. "Wouldn't miss it for the world," Eric's voice replied. Eric picked up his phone and placed it in his pocket; Marshall did the same. Without another word, Marshall quickly walked through the maze of bookcases and stepped out of the shop into the sweltering February heat.

4

Marshall felt the weight of the phone in his hand, which was much heavier and thicker than the one he had now. He tapped the screen. Nothing happened. *It's broken. Of course it's broken.* He felt a sudden, momentary wave of relief. *Maybe that's for the best. I should get rid of this thing. I should turn that old man in. I could be a hero!* Marshall thought. But as the thought crossed his mind, he knew it was not true. *They'll erase him. But they'll erase me too. They say the Resistance doesn't exist. If I met one of them, then I can't exist anymore either.*

He felt around the side and found a few buttons. *Perhaps it's off,* he thought curiously. Marshall had never had a phone that turned off before. He held each button down for a second until the phone screen lit up. He breathed a deep but quiet sigh. After a few moments, a series of unfamiliar icons appeared on the screen in a grid formation: a grey box with what appeared to be gears in it labeled "settings," a calculator icon, a blue box with a strange rectangular shape in the middle labeled "mail," a green box with another unfamiliar shape in it labeled "phone," a camera icon, and a white and yellow colored box labeled "notes." His own phone had no icons at all but instead responded only to voice commands.

There was a time set at the top left of the screen of the ancient phone, but it was completely off from the actual time.

First, Marshall tapped on the settings icon. He noticed immediately that almost all the settings were turned off: Wi-Fi, Bluetooth, and Cellular. He was not sure what any of these things were, but he guessed that keeping them off is what kept Skeyelink from accessing the phone. A spike of panic struck his stomach. He nervously tried to exit the settings for fear of accidentally switching one of the toggles to "on" but could not figure out how to do it, so he held the button on the side to turn the phone off.

Recognizing that he had already taken longer to inspect this phone than his normal shower would take, Marshall thought for a moment where he should hide it. Marshall opened the vanity doors below the sink. Behind the sink bowl there was a small lip against the back wall. Marshall carefully placed the phone on that lip and leaned it forward against the backside of the sink. He backed up and looked carefully to see if he could see it. It was well hidden, he decided. He then hopped in the shower, rinsed off quickly, and got out. Any extreme deviation beyond one's standard pattern could be picked up and flagged by Skeyelink. Marshall never knew when or if Skeyelink was listening, so it was always safer to assume Skeyelink was always listening.

Skeyelink connected all electronic devices to the central internet hub. Like an octopus with infinite tentacles, Skeyelink spread across the entire country, reached into every home, every office, every pocket, and tethered every device to itself. It was through Skeyelink that all information was shared and kept, all transactions were done, all important announcements were made, and all the movements and activities of citizens were tracked—for everyone's safety, of course.

He got dressed, went into the kitchen to heat up a standard dinner ration, which included all the essential nutrients as dictated by the Holy American President, who was an expert in human nutrition. Today's meal was a spongy meatloaf with watery gravy, diced rubbery carrots, and grainy mashed potatoes. Ten seconds in the Plasmaheat and his meal came out steaming hot. He grabbed the disposable tray, which itself was cool to the touch, poured himself a glass of water and sat down on the couch. He turned on the television, as all good Americans did over dinner, and began eating, masticating his sustenance without pleasure or thought. The meatloaf, which tasted much like the chicken he ate the day before, rolled over his tongue and down his gullet without much fanfare. His eyes stared blankly at the President's Evening News as it ran through all the president's accomplishments of the day, most of which had already been posted to everyone's phone on Facts throughout the day. The Holy American President had had a busy day: he had negotiated a new military partnership with the United States' closest ally,

The United Russian Republics, known as the URR; personally oversaw the capture and immolation of a terrorist cell in Wichita, Kansas; and won the Pebble Beach Pro-Am golf tournament despite being down nine shots at the beginning of the day. The newscasters praise of these accomplishments and unbelievable comeback filtered in and out of Marshall's ear canals.

The news anchor suddenly broke from what he had been saying. "We're going live now to our weekly address from the Holy American President's chief of staff, Mr. Mylnere."

The camera cut to the image of a balding man with a preternaturally pale pallor and a thin face, which ended at a pointed chin. Despite his unintimidating appearance, the instant his face popped onto the screen, Marshall innards were overcome with dread. Mylnere, the Holy American President's chief advisor and the leader of HALE, was commonly known as the man behind all of the erasures.

"My fellow Americans," Mylnere began. "First, I want to congratulate the Holy American President for all the amazing accomplishments he has achieved. He has saved our country repeatedly from the invasion of the Third World. It's always been clear that if you import the Third World, you become the Third World. Well, we have done the opposite. We have deported the Third World. We have rid ourselves of almost all the Third World trash that had been dumped on us for decades and we have become the greatest nation in the history of the world because of it.

"But that does not mean we can become complacent, which is why I come to you today. Despite all his courageous, selfless acts, the Holy American President can only do so much.

"I'm sure you have all heard by now of the vicious attack that took place earlier today. An innocent family was butchered by these devils, who should never have been here in the first place. Now, I want you all to be assured that the Holy American President is doing everything possible to ascertain how they got into the country and where they came from.

"I personally guarantee that their entire godforsaken country will pay for what these people have done. One of ours, all of yours!

"But in the meantime, we are counting on every single one of you, patriotic Americans, to keep an eye out for anything fishy and immediately report anyone who appears suspicious, especially those that look like they don't belong here. The Holy American President has declared that there will be a $100,000 reward for any tips that lead to an arrest.

"Thank you and may God bless America and may God bless the Holy American President."

The screen cut back to the news anchor, who began summarizing Mylnere's announcement.

Marshall's mind drifted from the screen and began churning through what he should do with his ancient phone.

His first thought was to store pictures and videos on it. A record of himself for someone in the future in case, or inevitably when, he was erased. But the best he could do there was take self-portraits of himself in his own bathroom. He did not dare bring the illegal phone outside of his apartment, let alone take pictures of himself or anything else in public.

He thought for a fleeting moment that he could somehow store evidence of the people he erased at work. If he could somehow keep their photographs on this phone, he could keep them alive in a way. He immediately thought of the woman in the blue dress with the dark curly hair. It had been months since her file came across his display, but he found he could not stop his mind from wandering back to her. Like the center of an inescapable hedge maze, all his thought paths eventually, no matter how much meandering, led to her. If only he could have kept just one photograph of her outside of his mind and memory, perhaps that would have been enough to have kept her alive somehow. It was too late for her, but maybe someone else? But no. There was no way to get this phone into the building, much less into his cubicle. There was no way to transfer the photos without taking the phone out and taking photos of the display. And there was no way he would survive the day if he even tried such a seditious act. The thought, the hope, the wish flared in his mind like ignited flash-paper and disappeared just as quickly.

In the end he decided he would use it as a diary of sorts. A place to store his thoughts that he knew he could never share with anyone else. To what end, he was not sure. Most likely no one would ever read anything he wrote down. Or if someone did find it, they'd probably destroy it immediately for fear of even holding such treasonous material. But at least it felt like he was doing something, anything, beyond what his life had been for over three decades now.

He finished his dinner, turned off the television, placed his tray in the trash and the glass in the dishwasher, and went to the bathroom to seemingly get ready for bed. Marshall figured he could use the phone whenever he could convincingly be on the toilet. Any more time spent in the bathroom might become suspicious. He reached behind the sink, pulled out the phone, and then began brushing his teeth as loudly as he could as he turned the phone on. The screen lit up and the same icons as before showed on the display. He tapped on the notes icon and began a new note as he finished brushing his teeth. He then pulled down his pants, sat on the toilet and typed in:

```
February 22nd, 2084
```

He paused, not knowing what else to write. And then realized that was as good a place as any.

```
I'm not sure what to write here or who
I'm writing to, if anyone. I guess I'm
writing to myself.
```

Marshall took a breath and looked at the phone. It felt like a momentous thing he had just done, placing thoughts down in a place that Skeyelink could not see. An inkling of pride slipped into his chest cavity before it occurred to him that this was all happening while he sat alone with his bare bottom on a porcelain toilet. The pride was instantly pushed out by his more natural state of fear and self-degradation. And suddenly it all came flooding out. His thumbs whirled as his mind rambled onto the screen like a river breaching a long-held levy.

There is something wrong with this world. Something terrible, awful, inhumane. Of all the people I've ever met, am I the only one to see it? Well, me and Mr. Blaire that is. Can it be just the two of us? No one else feels this terrible, aching, crush of life? If you can call this life. But what else is there? This is all I know. This is all anyone knows. Is there anything else? Everywhere else is worse than here. That's what the president tells us. He's always right, isn't he? Everywhere else is a shithole country, right? But how can they be worse than this?

But no one else says anything. I don't say anything. So maybe others feel it too. Or maybe it's just me and Eric. Maybe we're the crazy ones. Maybe everyone else's smile is real, is genuine. But no, that cannot be. I cannot believe that. There is something wrong with this world and they are hiding it from us.

Everyday I go in and I erase people. That can't be normal right? That can't be how it's always been. But we can't say

anything. If I say anything I'll be the
next one to be erased.

Marshall paused for a moment and then typed in the thought, the feeling, that he had been trying to ignore for his entire life.

I'm scared. And I'm alone.

Starting at the age of seven, Marshall had lived in terror, housed in a Presidential Care and Rehabilitation Facility in an old, converted school building with hundreds of other boys whose parents had also been erased. It was a terror he could see in the eyes of every other child in the facility. Over time, the fear slowly eased away from his conscious self and slipped into the background; but like a silent and malicious puppet master, it still subtly held sway over every moment, every decision, every thought Marshall had until his fear became embedded into the very fabric of his being.

Until that moment, Marshall had subconsciously done all he could to avoid acknowledging his constant dread. Now, sitting on his toilet, silently clutching a device that would assuredly lead to his own death, he embraced it. He stopped fighting against it. He stopped ignoring it. He let it overwhelm him. And then it passed. He shut the phone down and closed his eyes for a moment. His whole body was consumed with a feeling somewhere between relief, horror, and satisfaction.

Marshall stood up, pulled up his pants, flushed the toilet, and walked over to the sink to wash his hands. He then opened the cabinet doors of the cheap, plywood bathroom vanity and placed the phone behind the sink. Marshall then went back into his bedroom, laid down in his bed, and fell asleep.

That night he dreamt he was a child standing in a white hallway. His nose was assaulted by an overwhelming smell of ammonia and fear. He was crying, but he was not sure why. A man at the end of the hall, whom he thought was someone important, was screaming. He could not clearly make out his face but his voice sounded familiar.

"SOMEBODY HELP HER!"

A man in a white coat walked up to the screaming man and placed a hand on his shoulder, shaking his head. Despite being at the other end of the hallway and whispering, Marshall could hear the man clearly, as if he was whispering into Marshall's ear: "I'm sorry, there's nothing we can do. She has an ectopic pregnancy. I could lose my license. I could go to jail."

The screaming man shoved the man in the white coat and suddenly was overwhelmed by three men in dark black uniforms.

"GET OFF ME!" The man screamed. "THEY'RE KILLING HER!"

But the men did not get off. They held him down until he was subdued. Marshall stood there, thinking he should help, thinking something was wrong, but he was frozen.

A window appeared next to him that was not there a moment ago. He looked inside and there was a bed with the shape of a woman under a white blanket, partially stained red, lying on it.

He turned around and he was on the sidewalk. The man at the end of the hallway was with him. He looked up but could not see his face. It was a warm day and there were many people walking up and down the sidewalk around them. In front was an ice cream stand. The man looked down at Marshall. Despite not being able to make out his face, Marshall could tell he was attempting to smile as he handed Marshall a cone of strawberry ice cream. Marshall felt himself smile back at the man and then took a lick. The taste was exquisite. Sweet and slightly tangy. He felt the cool texture of the ice cream dissolve in his mouth and relished it. He looked up as the man took out his phone to pay.

Suddenly, six men carrying large, torso length weapons, wearing black masks and black Kevlar armor with the letters HALE across the front approached them. As soon as they appeared, people began walking quickly away from the spot. The man froze. Marshall grabbed his hand and started to pull but the man did not respond. They grabbed the man and spun him around to face Marshall as they handcuffed his hands behind his back. Marshall looked up into the man's face but could only see his eyes, which held no fear, no terror, only sadness. "I'm sorry," the man said, right before he was struck in the stomach by one of the uniformed men. Another placed a black cloth bag over his head and then he was gone.

Marshall awoke the next morning in a cold sweat. Fear and panic coursing through his veins. It was a dream he has had many times, but as usual, he was unable to recall any of it.

5

February 23rd, 2084

I could barely focus today. So many files to get through. There's no chance I hit my target efficiency today. Mr. Reeves is definitely going to talk to me if I don't do better tomorrow. He'll probably ask me "what did you accomplish this week?" before he erases me. But how can I with all the nonsense Eric fed me. The Resistance! I don't know what to believe. The whole idea is preposterous. The President has said so many times that it's a myth. No one is against him. Poll after poll show his approval ratings are at least 100%! Some months 200%, 300%, 400% approval! He's won every single election in my lifetime! How can there be a resistance?

Then again, how could there not be? There is something wrong with this world, and Eric proved to me yesterday that I'm not the only one that thinks so. It can't just be the two of us. There must be others. Maybe The Resistance does exist. But even if it does exist, what could I do to help? What can anyone do? One word, one toe out of line and I'll be the one being erased.

I probably shouldn't even be writing on this phone. I should just find a way to destroy it, get rid of it. Throw it away and never go back to that damn antique store. How dare he rope me into this? I'm probably already dead. They probably already know.

Marshall shut the phone down, pulled up his pants, flushed the toilet and went over to the vanity to hide the phone behind the sink.

The rest of the week went by without incident. Marshall woke up every morning, went to work, did his job, came home, ate his standard dinner ration over the President's evening news and went to sleep.

He was tempted to grab the phone from under the sink each night before bed. Writing on the phone brought him a great deal of anxiety and fear, as one feels when being pulled to the top of a rollercoaster; each click of the track, each type of a word bringing the rider, and the writer, one step closer to the drop. Yet there was a thrill about it that he found hard to resist. Not only did he fear the drop, he wanted it. He needed it. His life had been a perpetual walk around an even circular track. He had kept his head down and plodded along in the same lane for the last twenty-eight years. For the first time since he was placed in the Presidential Care and Rehabilitation Facility, Marshall felt a desire to leap off the path that was placed in front of him, to face his fear and even embrace it. He acknowledged for the first time since childhood that he felt and thought things that he was not supposed to feel or think, and he wanted to share them with someone or something, even if that thing was an inanimate object living behind his bathroom sink. But that feeling was fleeting. The temptation each night to take out the phone and write down his thoughts was overcome, wrestled into submission, by the fear that resided at the back of his throat. And so each night Marshall reluctantly went to bed without touching the phone.

Each night, Marshall dreamed of the woman with black curly hair. She never spoke, but she was always there. He dreamed of her standing in a doorway that led out to a patio overlooking the ocean, wearing a long flowing peach colored dress. He dreamed of her sitting at a small kitchen table wearing an olive-green t-shirt and oversized khaki pants, smiling at him as she ate her breakfast, a steaming hot cup of coffee sitting beside a plate of eggs and toast on the table in front of her. One night he dreamed of her at a playground, dark sunglasses sat above a large, joyful, love-filled smile.

The sunglasses obscured her eyes, but he could tell she was intently watching a child playing on the jungle gym.

Each dream gave Marshall a deep feeling of warmth, of belonging, like a lost dog reunited with his owner. He was excited to see her, just to be near her. It was not a sexual excitement, or a romantic one. Her presence was soothing, like the sun breaking through a cold, overcast day. Marshall simply yearned to sit next to her, to talk to her. But each time he chose not to. Not for fear or trepidation, but simply because he knew she was not his, or he was not hers, and so he was content just to see her, to be near her.

Each morning, he awoke to the bare, off-white walls of his bedroom with an emptiness within, knowing that she was not there. He wished he could stay in the dream, stay in the warmth of her presence. But he knew she would never live in his waking hours. He had erased her and erasure was permanent. So each morning he put on a pair of khaki pants, a white button up dress shirt, one of his five ties, his brown Oxford shoes, and trudged off to the Agency of Historical Accuracy.

* * *

That Sunday, Marshall woke up at seven o'clock as he did every Sunday. He was assigned the eight o'clock mass. Marshall showered, got dressed, ate a standard breakfast ration of scrambled eggs and sausages, both of which tasted remarkably like salted, soggy cardboard, and made his way to the Church of the Holy American President, which was seven blocks away.

It was warm outside and the air was thick, like walking through steam coming off a bowl of soup. As he got closer to the church, he began to see the familiar fair-skinned faces of the congregation. This was one of the few places Marshall frequented where he consistently saw women and children. The Save America's Families act of 2049 ensured women were given the opportunity to fulfill their God given role of raising children by keeping them out of careers that might distract them from motherhood. Since Marshall spent most of his time in a government building or at home, he only consistently saw women at service.

He had also decided long ago that he would never marry, never have children, even though it was every citizen's patriotic duty to produce at least three children, in order to replace the less desirable, darker population that had been erased. He could not bear the idea of being erased and leaving behind people that depend on him. Plus, life was simpler this way. He did not need or want the complications that came with Family and Spousal Registration, Presidential Fidelity camps for children, and all the other responsibilities that the President placed on heads of households. So instead, for a couple hours every Sunday, Marshall enjoyed watching the women in their Sunday dresses tending to their children, imagining what it might be like to have a family of his own.

When he reached the towering stone church, there was a line of people waiting to check in and go through security. He scanned the crowd of people, hoping not to see Michael Black Cain. Those that were not actively going through security mostly had their heads down, eyes glued to their phones. Michael Black Cain was no where in sight.

Marshall never missed a service, even when he felt ill. It was easier to make it through a service feeling unwell, than to complete the paperwork and go through the interview necessary to excuse an absence.

Marshall fell into line behind a picturesque family of five. The father, in a dark blue suit, paisley tie, and an American Flag pin affixed proudly to his lapel, smiled and nodded to other men in the crowd. He stood tall and proud behind his blond haired, slim figured wife, who was on one knee talking to their three children, two boys and a girl between the ages of five and nine. The boys wore dark blue suits to match their father, and the girl wore a white dress with a yellow flower pattern to match her mother. Marshall watched as the mother shepherded the three children forward, shushing them each time they began to talk or ask questions, until they arrived at front of the line where large, masked men in black police gear and sunglasses waved each parishioner through body scanners, while facial recognition cameras captured the image of each citizen.

Marshall then stepped through security, his arms raised over his head as a HALE agent watched an image of his x-rayed body walk past, and then past the giant wooden doors into the church itself.

The nave stretched out about two hundred feet in front of him with wooden pews on either side. Tall doric columns, each adorned with an American flag that hung over the center pews, reached for the expansive vault of the church.

Straight ahead in the apse hung a large full-length portrait of the Holy American President, standing in a navy-blue suit, white shirt, and blood red tie. His face was stern and imposing and in his right hand, held up next to his head, was a leather-bound bible, the American flag etched into the base of the cover peeking out behind his abnormally large thumb. On one side of the portrait hung a crucifix made of wood. Jesus's emaciated alabaster body hung limply, his face, with an adoring expression, pointed towards the portrait in the center. On the other side of the portrait stood a statue of the Virgin Mary, draped in blue and white. Her face also adoringly transfixed towards the Holy American President.

Marshall walked up the center aisle to his assigned pew in row twenty-eight. He was grateful that he was assigned an aisle seat. The pews slowly filled in and at eight o'clock sharp the congregation rose and Pastor Chilkir walked out onto the stage. As always, Pastor Chilkir was dressed in an expensive, impeccably tailored suit. He wore navy blue slacks, shiny hazelnut shoes, and a sky-blue button-up dress shirt beneath a matching navy-blue blazer, upon which an American flag was pinned. He held a leatherbound bible in one hand.

Pastor Chilkir smiled out at the crowded church, his immaculate teeth white and glistening. His hair was perfectly combed to one side. He raised his arms and looked over the crowd.

"Good morning!" He started. His voice was flowed silkily out of his mouth, straight into the ears of his expectant flock.

"What a wonderful morning it is! The sun is shining, the birds are chirping, and our great, great country is booming with success after success! God is good and the president is great!"

"God is good and the president is great," the congregation repeated.

"Please, sit, sit, sit."

The church echoed with the sound of a thousand souls sitting down simultaneously. It was at this point in the service that Marshall's mind always began to wander. This particular Sunday, his mind was full of contradiction and confusion as his desires battled with his fears. He had held strong ever since Wednesday night and resisted taking out the phone, even though he was drawn to the rebellious freedom he felt when inscribing his thoughts on it. One thing had been pestering him all week: Eric's question. He had tried not to think about it but in that moment, staring up at the altar, at the portrait of the Holy American President, at Jesus and the Virgin Mary, Marshall's mind began to churn.

Do I like my job? Of course I don't like my job. Does anyone like their job? But I need to eat, to pay my rent, what else am I going to do? It's not like I can leave my job anyway. No one quits being an Eraser. You're an Eraser until you're erased. Everyone knows this.

"Alright, we have a reading from Leviticus this morning," Pastor Chilkir smiled. Marshall tried to pay attention to the reading, which he had heard many times before, but his attention drifted in and out between his own thoughts and the words blaring out of the speakers.

If I'm to be honest with myself, I hate my job. I can't stand it. At one time I felt disgusted by it. But now? Now I feel nothing. And I hate that too.

"...do not take your wife's.."

How many people have I erased over the years? Thousands? Tens of thousands? Let me see...I probably finish on average two files a day. That's twelve a week...

"...that is detestable..."

I get a week off for Christmas and a week off for the President's birthday so that's fifty weeks...that's about six hundred a year, eighteen years...that's over ten thousand! Marshall's stomach began to heave like a boat adrift in the open ocean.

"This is God's word!" The pastor concluded.

"Amen!" someone a few rows behind Marshall called out.

"Amen," Marshall absentmindedly whispered a second later.

"Now let's head over to Gensis, shall we?"

Thirty thousand...How is that even possible? Marshall had never thought much about his job before. Better not to think about it. Keep your head down and plod along was always his way.

"And Hamm, the father of Canaan..."

If I've erased ten thousand on my own...how many have been erased in total? I cannot believe...

"...and knew what his youngest son had done..."

I can't. I can't go back. I can't keep erasing people.

"Cursed be Canaan; a servant of servants..."

The woman with the dark curly hair found her way into his mind. He felt the sudden urge to cry. He took three long quiet breaths to steady himself, careful to keep his eye glued to the lector in front of him.

"Can I get an Amen?" The pastor yelled out fervently.

"Amen," Marshall's mumble was drowned out by the rest of the voices, which were loud, clear, and crisp. He continued trying to compose himself, fully aware of the cameras hidden around the entire church; Skeyelink was always present. He watched the priest walk up to the altar, and held up a large, leather-bound bible, identical to the one held by the Holy American President in the portrait behind him. Marshall stood with the rest of the flock, making a small cross symbol with his thumb over his forehead, lips, and then heart.

"I have one more for you this morning. A reading from Matthew," he began. Marshall tried to focus on the reading. "Hearing that Jesus had silenced the Sadducees, the Pharisees got together..." the priest read. The image of the woman with the black curly hair flashed into Marshall's mind again.

Why can't I stop thinking about her? Marshall closed his eyes for a moment, trying to wrestle his thoughts from her grasp.

"...which is the greatest commandment..."

She's gone. Erased. As I will be if I stop showing up to work. They'll find me and I'll be erased within an hour.

"Love the Lord your God...:"

Maybe that wouldn't be the worst thing. The thought was sharp and sudden, like a knife in the dark. It shocked Marshall. He had always feared erasure, immolation, death in any form. Never had he invited it in. The thought came as if whispered by someone else into his ear, rather than from within himself.

"...and greatest commandment. And the second..."

Yes. I'll be erased eventually. No eraser escapes it. It could be today, it could be tomorrow, it could be fifty years from now. Fifty years...if I'm still living this life in fifty years they might as well erase me now.

The pastor then closed the bible.

"And all of God's people said?" He called out.

"Amen!" The congregation called back, and then they all sat back down as the priest took a breath before he began.

"What does our Lord mean when he says 'Love your neighbor?' And why does he demand we love God first? Does he want us to love everyone equally?"

"NO!" cried a voice from the back.

The priest smiled. "Correct. Of course not. If he did, he would have said 'love everyone as yourself.' No, our lord is very clear here. Love your neighbor. God first, then neighbor. Love the higher power, then the ones who are your neighbors, the ones near you, the ones who live close to you. Love the higher power first! God, and our President, the highest power in our land."

"God bless the President," the faithful chanted.

"God bless the President!" The priest cried out. "And then, after loving the higher power, love those close to you, not just close to you in location, but close to you in spirit, close to you in blood! We do not choose our neighbors! God chose our neighbors! He shows each and every one of you who your neighbors are right before your eyes! Your neighbors are those that share your ancestry, those that share your kinship, those that share your language! How can you be neighbors with someone who doesn't speak English! You can't! You can't be neighbors with someone you can't communicate with! You can't be neighbors with barbarians from other places who once invaded these lands to try and destroy our way of life! Those are not your neighbors! Look around, everyone please, look to your left and to your right."

Marshall looked over the gallery of porcelain visages, observing everyone looking at one another and affirming their own membership in this heaven-blessed brotherhood.

There is something wrong with this world. And I think Eric can explain it to me. They're going to erase me anyway. What do I have to lose?

"You see? These are the neighbors our loving God has given us. These are the neighbors our loving President allowed to stay in this great, beautiful country God has given us!"

"God bless the President!" The flock cheered loudly.

"God bless the President," Marshall said halfheartedly, then he noticed the man in the pew across the aisle from him glancing at him. It was the same man from line with the dark navy suit and the American flag pin.

"Our wonderful, loving President has expelled the terrorists! Expelled the heathens! Expelled the barbarians! Our wonderful loving President, whose life God himself saved from certain death all those years ago, was gifted to us by the Lord almighty to save this wonderful country of ours!"

"GOD BLESS THE PRESIDENT!" Marshall bellowed with the crowd, consciously avoiding eye contact with the man across the aisle.

6

The following Tuesday after work, Marshall shuffled into Blaire's antique store. Eric stood behind the counter and smiled.

"Good afternoon, Marshall. Coffee?"

"Yes, please."

They stepped through the store into the backroom, where the voice box was already set up. Eric turned it on. Marshall and Eric quietly placed their phones on the table next to the voice box.

"So, how's business this week?" Marshall's voice came out of the device.

"Slow, as always, but that's okay," Eric's voice replied. Then the sound of mugs being brought out and a coffee maker starting up emanated from the box. Eric led Marshall through the backdoor, down the stairs, and into the small art gallery.

Marshall was not sure how to start or what to say so he began glancing at the art on the walls.

"You painted all these?" he asked.

"No, not all. Most. But not all. Some of these are posters, prints. There's a couple photographs as well."

They walked together around the room and Marshall stopped at a framed poster. It had a circle split into different colored stripes against a black background. A pigeon with a camera for a head stood in the middle of the circle and white lettering above.

Marshall heard Eric chuckle. "That's from before you were born, but it was funny at the time."

"What's this one?" Marshall pointed to a black and white photograph in a simple black frame of a man in a white shirt and dark pants holding what appeared to be a grocery bag. He stood in the middle of a street in front of four tanks, lined up in single file.

"That? That's Tiananmen Square. China. 1989. That man stopped a line of tanks all by himself."

"Who was he?"

"No one knows for sure."

Marshall took a few more steps to his left and stopped in front of a painting of what appeared to be the inside of a barn. Farm animals lined the edge of the barn, all looking at a fat pig, sitting on top of a box wearing olive green clothes. He appeared to be addressing the crowd of animals.

"One of yours?"

"Mmhmm," Eric nodded.

Next to that painting was a print of a man cut off right below the shoulders. He had a stern face, and a mustache, but was also wearing earrings, a violet top, and a gold crown. The words "God Save The Queen" were printed across the bottom.

"Why? Why do you have these?"

"These are all reminders, Marshall. Some are glimpses of the past. Some are pictures of the present, in a way. But they're all reminders of what we're doing. What we're fighting for and fighting against. A reminder that one person can make a difference. One man can stop four tanks. All it takes is courage and sacrifice."

"Reminders? That's worth the risk? If they find these..."

"Then I'm dead. But like I said last week, we're all dead anyway. What matters is what we leave behind."

"Are you the head of The Resistance?"

A chuckle escaped Eric's lips. "No, Marshall. There is no head. I don't even know most of the people in The Resistance. I'm a recruiter. I'm the front door. I lay the foundation, tell you what this is all about."

"How many people have you recruited?"

"Not sure...a couple dozen I'd guess over the years."

"Does everyone you try to recruit join The Resistance?"

"No, not everyone. Most never make it into the back room for coffee! Some promising candidates I've had to give up on over the years. Just a few. But everyone that's made it down here has joined. I'm a good judge of character, you see. All those coffees we had over those months, that was your interview. I knew right away you had a moral compass when you came back and paid for that watch. And I could tell from our conversations that you recognize something doesn't make sense about our country, even though you wouldn't say so."

"How'd you know I'd come back after last week?"

"You took the phone. You put it in your pocket. That's how. Did you write in it?"

"Um, yes. A couple of things. How'd you know?"

"Well, that's really all you can do with it. We live in a world where we have to censor every word out of our mouths, even sensor our thoughts. Humans aren't born to live like that, and when given a chance, those thoughts and feelings we're forced to bury will always come out. It's in our nature to share information, even if it's with no one in particular." Eric gestured to the armchairs in the center of the room. "Please, have a seat. I'll be right back."

Eric went through another door in the back of the room as Marshall sat down. A few minutes later, Eric came out with two steaming hot mugs of coffee.

"You didn't think I'd let you leave without a cup of your favorite coffee, did you?" He smiled and winked at Marshall as he handed him the mug. Marshall took a deep breath through his nose, inhaling the smell deep into his soul. Eric sat down next to him.

"So, where should we begin? At the beginning I would suppose. Always begin at the beginning. You're probably trying to figure out, what is The Resistance? We're the ones fighting against the evil of the president. We're the ones fighting to try and bring this country back to what it once was, a country built on democracy, on self-determination, on liberty." Eric paused for a moment and took a sip of his coffee. Marshall followed suit. "Do you know how the president became the president?"

"Of course. Everyone knows that story."

"Tell me how."

"Our country was failing. Falling apart. We were being overrun by terrorists and gangs and horrible, horrible people. People were flooding into this country, killing Americans, stealing from them. They were eating our pets! He didn't want to be president, but everyone demanded he run, and he won every single state that year. It only took him three months to get rid of all the invaders. Sent them all back to their home countries. And so he saved America. He's won every election ever since."

"Yes, of course. That's the story we're all taught in school. It's the only story you can find when you look it up in the digital library. None of it is true."

"None of it? What do you mean? That can't be right. All the old copies of the President's Daily, the news broadcasts, all the Facts posts...you can see all of them."

"Where, Marshall, *where* can you see all of them?"

Marshall reached for his phone, before realizing it was upstairs listening to the voice box.

Eric nodded to Marshall's pocket. "Exactly. You were born in what, forty-eight?" Marshall nodded. "That's sixteen years after the Great Digitization. So, you've never held a book, a newspaper, or a magazine in your entire life. Everything you've ever been taught, and everything that proves those things are correct come through Skeyelink. And all of it, every word, every picture, is controlled by the president. Did you know before you were born there were actually many newspapers, many news stations, and thousands of journalists in this country?"

Marshall shook his head. "No. I...there's only the President's Daily, and of course what he posts on Facts."

"One of their key jobs was to report on what those in power were doing, so that they could be held accountable. And it was one of the first things the president went after. He attacked journalists relentlessly, turning the public's trust against true journalists. We lost one of our most important checks on his power when he did that. People that followed him decided what he said was true and that journalists, experts, scientists, historians, and anyone who said anything that didn't line up with his mad rantings were all lying or part of some vast conspiracy against the American people."

Eric paused for a moment and then shifted gears. "Have you ever heard the phrase 'money is power?' "

Marshall shook his head.

"It's a phrase people knew and understood a long time ago. They've eliminated that phrase, and even that concept completely so people wouldn't catch on to what they've done. But that is the crux behind all of this. Behind how our entire country is run. The people who have the most wealth are the ones that have all the power. The ones that make the laws. The ones that run HALE. The ones that erase people who resist. That is how this country went from a functioning democracy to what it is today. Let me ask you another question. What does it mean to be rich?"

"Rich? It means you have a lot of money. Like a hundred million dollars."

"Wrong, Marshall. Having a lot of money doesn't make one rich. Having a lot *more* money than everyone else; that's what makes one rich. You can be rich with only a hundred dollars, as long as everyone else has only one dollar."

"Right, okay. That makes sense."

"So, if wealth is not based on how much money one has but based on how much more money one has than others, then there's two ways to become rich: accumulate your own wealth and make sure no one else accumulates wealth. Really, the best way is to do both at the same time. My father explained all this to me when I was a child. The rich in this country had been working on a plan for decades to gain control of the country and all the wealth. About sixty years ago—I was only eleven at the time—all their plans came to a head. The president became president by convincing half the country that the reason they were struggling was because of poorer people from other countries. He, along with a vast media machine, convinced his followers that poorer people were coming to take the last bit of wealth that poor Americans had left. They even convinced them that all these people coming in from other countries were evil, murderers and rapists. In reality, struggling Americans were poor because the billionaires of the time, now trillionaires, had taken all the wealth from this country and hoarded it for themselves. They had hoarded so much wealth that the rest of the country couldn't even fathom how much money they had. But it was easier for Americans to believe that poor foreigners were to blame than wealthy

Americans. Meanwhile, they made sure that the rest of America worked for just enough money to survive."

"I don't understand. People believed poorer people were to blame?"

Eric thought for a moment. Then he continued, "Close your eyes, Marshall."

Marshall quickly shut his eyes.

"Now picture a kitchen. A nice, American kitchen, with an island in the middle. Around this island stands about twenty people. Do you see them?"

"Yes, I see them."

"Now before I continue, let me ask you this: how many people around your imaginary island are not white?"

"None," Marshall said quickly.

"Of course not. Because that is the America the president wants you to believe in. Those are the people that you've been taught are the only true Americans. Now, in the middle of the island is a large apple pie, cut into twenty slices. Enough for everyone."

"Sounds delicious."

"It is. Best apple pie you've ever seen. Now one man steps forward and takes eighteen pieces for himself."

"Well that's not fair."

"No, it's not. The other nineteen people cry foul. Why does he get so much? It leaves only two pieces for everyone to share! But the man looks at them all, and then quietly points to the window. In the window is a family with darker skin, and they're hungry. They're looking into the kitchen and it's clear they want some pie. And the man with the eighteen pieces of pie points to them and he says, 'see those people who don't look like you, who are not from this house? They're here to steal these last two pieces of pie. If you don't get enough pie, it's because of them."

"That's what happened?"

"Essentially."

"And everyone believed him?"

"No. A lot of people saw through this lie. But enough people believed him that he was able to win the presidency. Twice."

"Why? How come so many people believed him?"

"There were many reasons. First, there was the sheer volume of lies he told. It was impossible to fact check all of them because it was so constant. And the lies were so outlandish they became commonplace in a way. He and his spokespeople gaslit the country over and over again, telling everyone two plus two makes five, and his followers became so used to this that they became accustomed to trusting what they were told over what they saw or knew in their hearts."

"Gaslit?"

"Yeah, telling people their own experiences are false. Believe me, and not your own eyes. People's lives were getting worse, and they'd say 'your life is better now than ever.' You could see a video of an innocent woman being gunned down by a HALE agent in the middle of the street and they'd tell you she was attacking the officers, that the murder was self-defense, when the video clearly shows it wasn't. Just constantly telling people two plus two makes five."

"Okay, I think I understand. He lied so much it became hard to tell the lies from the truth."

"Exactly. Those that were inclined to believe him from the beginning were now trapped in a world where either they keep believing his lies or face the reality that the entire world of fear and hatred he had built for them was a lie. Most weren't ready to do that until it was too late. And that brings me to the next reason: fear. Fear and anger. These are the basest of human emotions and the easiest to manipulate. People will do almost anything when they're afraid and angry. It's much harder to motivate people through love, compassion, and logic."

"I don't follow."

"Okay, let's try another exercise. Imagine you're standing in a room on the third floor of a building. There's only one stairway down and there's a huge fire standing between you and the exit. There's no way around it. But there's a window. The fire is coming closer. What would you do?"

"I'd probably jump out of the window."

"Right, most people would. Even if it means excruciating pain when you land. Now imagine the fire isn't on your floor, but someone runs upstairs and tells you the fire has consumed the bottom two floors, and that there's no way out. He shows you a video of someone burning to death and tells you that's what is happening downstairs. He tells you over and over and over again that you're in imminent danger, that the whole floor is about to collapse and you'll be immediately consumed by the fire below. Even if you can't see the fire, you can't smell it..."

"Okay, I understand. If he can make me believe the fire is just below my feet, that the floor is about to give way, I'd probably jump."

"Exactly. So, he yelled fire at every chance he got. He claimed the country was failing, turning into a third world country. He claimed that immigrants were invading the country and stealing from Americans, raping Americans, murdering Americans, and by Americans of course he meant white Americans. And people believed him. They believed there was an emergency, that the country was on fire, and they jumped. When the president became president, he ensured that every program the government had to help the poor was eliminated. He claimed that all of those programs were corrupt, were wrought with waste, fraud and abuse, and abolished them under the guise of saving the American taxpayer money. He wrestled power away from congress and…"

"What's congress?"

"This country used to have a body of representatives from each state that would pass laws."

"The president didn't pass laws?"

"Not for the first two hundred and fifty years of America's history, no. But the president took…well I should say the congressmen and women who were in the president's party allowed him to take all the power congress had."

"There were congress*women*?"

"Yes, women had the right to any job a man had, until about thirty-five years ago."

"And they just left their jobs?"

"Some fought back. I don't think you need more than one guess to figure out what happened to them."

"Erased." Marshall thought about the dark curly haired woman. *Maybe she fought back. Maybe she wanted to do something other than be a maid, or a secretary, or a mother. Maybe that's why she was erased.*

"Public immolations too. Do you know the history of your job? Do you know how the erasures began?"

Marshall shook his head.

"They weren't always called erasures. At first, they were called deportations. He started with the most vulnerable, the ones that he had blamed for all of America's problems. People who didn't speak English. People who were here without permission. People who looked different from you and me. People he claimed were terrorists. Back then, there was a law that said all people who live here, *all people*, have a right to a trial before a judge. It was in the Constitution, and it was called due process. He ignored that and began sending people out of the country into horrible prisons, basically torture camps, in other countries. Some people tried to stop him. Many people cheered him on. Most people sat on their hands and watched it happen while shaking their heads. But it kept happening until it became commonplace. Until people got used to it. Then he went after anyone who opposed him. He started with those who had power. First mayors, judges, lawyers, and journalists; then congressmen and governors, and anyone wealthy who did not bend the knee. He labeled them terrorists and they disappeared. Then he went after any citizen who spoke out against him. Soon, there was no one left who dared to speak out. It wasn't long after that they took control over the internet and…"

"The internet?"

"What you know now as Skeyelink. Before Skeyelink, there were many companies that you could pay to connect your phone and your home or your business to the internet. The president took over all these companies in the name of national security. He said he was an expert in hacking and cybersecurity and needed control to make sure the barbarian countries weren't infiltrating our data. Once they had control of all information flowing to people's devices, the next obvious step was to destroy any evidence of the past that did not follow the story they wanted to tell. That was the Great Digitization. Hailed as a wonder of the new technological age, and a necessity for national security, they made sure every single person was given devices connected to Skeyelink, controlled by Skeyelink. People traded in their phones, their computers, for brand new machines. They banned all devices that were not connected to Skeyelink. The punishment, of course, was erasure or public immolation."

Marshall immediately thought of the phone under his sink.

"Then they destroyed everything ever written on paper. Confiscated every painting, poster, and print. I remember that week. Zealous followers went into every library, every bookstore. People who did not turn out their own places had their homes ransacked. Skies across the country were blackened from the bonfires that spotted every city. It rained ash for days and the smell of burning paper stuck to all of us for months. But in the end, they accomplished what they set out to do. They claimed that nothing was lost. They claimed that everything had been digitized and was now reachable for free in the palm of your hand. But the reality? Millions of books were purged from the digital library. Newspapers shuttered and all their past articles were gone. Any trace of the past that did not support the president vanished. And that, Marshall, is the country we live in now."

"How? How was all this possible? How is it possible that I don't know any of this? That no one knows any of this? This can't be right."

"History is written by the victors. What you learned as a child, everything you learned in school on your deskscreens, at the PCRF, everything you read on your phone, everything coming out of your television, is the voice of the president. The ones that do know this, like myself, can't say a word. Who would believe us anyway? But if I said any of this to anyone, I'd probably appear on your screen at work the next day."

Marshall sat quietly for a moment, confused, trying to comprehend everything that Eric had just told him. But it was like trying to see out of a warped stained-glass window. None of it made sense against the backdrop of his own knowledge.

"I know that face," Eric said quietly. "I've seen it before. You're trying to somehow meld the stories together. It's natural to want to hold on to the world you know. It's okay. We're going to stop here for today. Don't try to make sense of it all at once. But now that you know the truth, you'll begin to see it everywhere you look. You've just been freed from the cave, and you'll see the shadows on the wall were never real. Do me a favor, when you have some time. Go out in the world, take a walk, leave your apartment, talk to some people, listen to the conversations around you. It will become obvious to you now that the veil has been lifted. By this time next week, it'll be so obvious that you'll wonder how come you never figured it out."

A silence fell over the room. Marshall, his mouth partially agape, stared at Eric's face. He could almost physically feel his mind fracturing, like lightning shaped cracks spreading over a pane of glass. On some level he knew and understood what Eric had told him was true. In fact, part of him felt as though he had always known. But he did not want to believe it. He felt an urge to run back up the stairs in the hopes that he would trip and wake up to find the past several months were a dream, that he had never had coffee with Eric, never even walked into Blair's Antiques. And he also felt a minutia of vindication, a satisfaction that his prior feelings, that there was something wrong with this world, were right all along.

Eric stood up and reached a hand out to Marshall to help him up. "Time to go home, Marshall. Try your best to go about your week like nothing has happened. When you're at home, take a few minutes to get your thoughts down on the phone. I always find my thoughts clarify themselves when I'm able to read them back to myself."

"Sure. Sure, okay. I'll..I'll try that."

"You know what you should also do? Take a walk to The Market."

"The Market?"

"Yes, Marshall, The Market."

"The Market is miles away!"

"Not if you walk the straight shot."

"You mean through Harmony Heights? And...and Elmwood Estates? Are you crazy?"

"No, I'm not crazy. Take a walk, Marshall." Marshall looked into the old man's face, on which a knowing smile was painted. "Trust me."

Marshall spent the walk home thinking trust was a feeling he may never feel again.

7

Over the next two days a fresh heatwave engulfed Washington. The air hung thick, heavy, and humid over the city, as if the streets themselves were caught wearing a suede coat in a summer storm. The earthy metallic smell of concrete when it first starts raining permeated every block, even though it had not rained in weeks.

Marshall felt as though the same thick haze that was infiltrating the city had also swamped the crevices of his brain. His thoughts felt slow and sluggish. Attempting to follow his own consciousness was like pulling tissue out of peanut butter.

Wednesday inched along ever so slowly as Marshall found he had to use all of his focus to simply keep his facial expressions neutral and his mind on his workstation screen. He worked through his lunch hour so as not to have to interact with anyone else in the building. He did not feel like he had the fortitude to maintain a conversation with another human being. Despite this, he barely completed one file that day.

On Thursday, however, Marshall decided to pause mid-file and go down to the lunchroom, simply to get away from what had become the unbearable task that was his job. As soon as he sat down with his standard lunch ration, he almost immediately regretted not skipping lunch as he had the day before. No sooner had he begun to pick up his turkey and cheese sandwich, which bore more resemblance to a drowned napkin topped with wet plastic, than Michael Black Cain walked over with his tray and sat down opposite him.

"Marshall! Where were you yesterday? You missed a lively discussion about the wondrous advancements we've made in medicine since the Holy American President saved our country!" Michael's enthusiasm was as potent as ever.

"Oh?" Marshall responded, attempting to demonstrate genuine interest in the words spewing from Michael Cain's face. "Why don't you fill me in."

"Well it's all things I'm sure you already know. We mostly talked about the miracle cure for homosexuality and our eradication of vaccine addiction. They said it couldn't be done, but our Holy President is a genius. The countless lives he has saved! Thank God they were able to invent that MedBed for him to keep him in tip top shape this whole time!"

Marshall took a large bite of his sandwich, filling his mouth beyond the ability to utter language, and nodded his head in agreement.

Michael Cain continued, "of course what brought this up was his announcement yesterday that they have finally found a cure for cancer. I'm sure you saw that on Facts Social."

Marshall had not, in fact, checked his Facts Social in several days, which at that moment he realized had been a mistake, as it was well known that they track who is keeping up with the Holy American President's messaging. Still chewing, Marshall vigorously nodded his head.

"Can you believe they've been testing for cancer wrong all these decades? Of course, he's been so busy fixing this country that he never had a chance to really look at cancer, even though he's one of the world's experts in the subject. No one knows medicine like he does! But one look at it and BANG, he found the problem. The testing was all wrong! Five thousand 'cancer patients,'" Michael created air quotations with his fingers as he spoke those words, "were given new tests, formulated by the President himself, and not a single one tested positive! The epidemic that was once cancer is officially gone, just like that!" Michael snapped his fingers loudly for emphasis.

"Talking about the cancer announcement, huh? Earth shattering, wasn't it?" The baritone voice of Trevor Penara, from the Agency of Labor and Statistics boomed over Marshall's shoulder.

"Trevor! Sit, sit. Yes, I was just catching Marshall up on our conversation yesterday," Michael gestured towards the seat across from him, inviting Trevor to sit his hulking frame next to Marshall.

"Wonderous time we live in, eh?"

"Wonderous!" Michael agreed.

Marshall finally swallowed his overly large bite and replied, "amazing times."

"New jobs report comes out tomorrow, by the way. I can't get into specifics of course, but I'll tell you this, the economy is booming! We added more jobs this month than in any other month in the history of this country! That's fifty-one consecutive months we've broken the record. It's unbelievable!"

"Unbelievable," Marshall replied automatically. As he said it though, he realized it was literally unbelievable. Every month for over four years, Trevor has given them the inside scoop that the country added more jobs that month than in any other month in history, and Marshall had accepted it as truth without hesitation. But in this moment he realized it was not possible. He took another bite of his soggy sandwich.

"Unemployment at nearly zero again," Trevor continued. "I mean the consistency of this economy really makes my job easy. The numbers wouldn't be this good even if I just made them up out of thin air!"

"Thanks be to the President!" Michael chimed in.

"Thanks be," Trevor and Marshall both responded programmatically.

"In other news," Michael said in a voice imitating a news anchor, "guess who's getting a promotion!" Michael pointed his thumb back at his own chest and exposed a grin that reeked of skin level self-assuredness.

"Congrats!" Trevor reached his hand over and Michael shook it with the enthusiasm of an overtired toddler.

"What's the new position?" Marshall asked, struggling with his entire being to feign interest and happiness for Michael.

"You're looking at the new Northeast Regional director of Spiritual Education. Basically, I'm now in charge of making sure all American students are being taught the right religion. We've made incredible headway into saving the souls of all Americans over the past few decades but there are still some people slipping through the cracks. But if we can make sure all the children are taught from an early age, there's less likelihood they'll end up as some sort of heathen when they grow up. Mark my words, the more God is in the schools, the less of these free-thinking terrorists we'll have in this country. Nothing stamps out dissent like a healthy dose of the fear of God."

"Hear, hear, spoken like a true patriot!" Trevor raised his glass of water and then quickly took a gulp.

"Congratulations, Michael," Marshall said. "You really deserve it."

"Thanks, Marshall. I definitely do. Been working my butt off but it has all been worth it. Now I get to be in a real position of influence, shaping the minds that are the softest and easiest to mold. I promise you I'll do everything in my power to make sure all Americans are fully instilled with the love of our savior and a burning hatred for all the false religions out there in the world.

"I have no doubt you'll succeed...for all of us," Marshall said, and then took the last bit of sandwich he had and shoved it into his mouth. He quickly chewed and swallowed and then stood up. "Well, I have to get back to work. The files just keep on coming."

"Of course. Keep up the good work," Michael said, nodding.

"See you," Trevor said as he began wolfing down his sandwich.

Marshall brought his empty tray back to the return window and placed it on the conveyor belt that brought it back to the kitchens. He then made his way back up to the fifth floor to finish his shift, hating every second he had to stay in that building.

* * *

When Marshall got back to Prospera Haven, he found Mrs. Johnson once again standing by her mailbox. She wore a poorly fitting, dark blue floral dress cut just below the knees, exposing dark varicose veins on her calves that looked like an old subway map. Her white hair flew haphazardly as if she just stepped out of a fast-moving boat on the open ocean. She held open the door, staring blankly at the brass back of the empty mailbox. She did not appear to have noticed him coming in and Marshall's first instinct was to try to sneak past her upstairs to avoid the interaction, but after three stealthy, catlike steps towards the stairs he paused.

"Mrs. Johnson?" Marshall said quietly.

Mrs. Johnson turned with a start, clearly startled by the sudden presence of another person, or perhaps by her own mind's sudden return to the present. Her eyes focused on Marshall, and she cracked a friendly glimmer of a smile.

"Oh, Marshall. Afternoon. How are you, my dear?"

"I'm fine, Mrs. Johnson. Are you alright?"

"Oh, oh yes. I'm okay, dear."

"Do you need help with something?"

"Oh, oh no. I'm okay, dear. But you're sweet for asking."

"Let me at least walk you to your apartment."

"Oh, I can manage. It's just right here down the hall."

Against every natural inclination in his body, and completely surprising to himself, Marshall took a few steps toward her. He heard himself say "I insist," and offered her his arm. She looked up at him with a face full of surprise and with a tinge of suspicion, but took his arm and began walking towards her apartment, two doors down the hall. Mrs. Johnson looked into the retinal scanner in the center of her door and the door slid open.

"Thank you dear," she said. Then, after a pause, "would you like to come in for a warm beverage?"

"Thank you, Mrs. Johnson, but…"

"Oh, please," she said in a kindly tone that straddled the border between pleading and asking. "Just one cup of coffee or tea." She paused for a moment, and then mimicking him added, "I insist."

"Okay, I guess I have time for a cup of something warm."

He stepped into an apartment that was identical to his in layout alone. Unlike Marshall's apartment, which was as sparsely furnished as was livable, Mrs. Johnson's was cluttered with myriad pieces of furniture that blended together like a conglomeration of random sparkly objects collected by a crow. None of the furniture matched and it took a surefooted walk to weave one's way around it all. Aside from an armchair that faced a wall mounted television screen, all of the furniture was covered with items of every kind. The apartment reminded Marshall in some ways of Blair's Antiques store, if the entire store had been picked up and shaken like a snow globe.

Marshall noticed that the windows were closed. The air inside was heavy, like a comforter on a hot day, and the smell of a damp carpet infiltrated Marshall's nose with reckless disregard. He found that his lungs immediately began laboring harder as his chest rose and fell visibly under his shirt, like an overworked bellows.

Mrs. Johnson shuffled over to the kitchen and filled a teapot with water.

"Please, sit," she instructed Marshall.

Marshall scanned the room, looking for a space to sit. He meandered over to what appeared to be a small white plastic table, which was covered by an avalanche of odds and ends that were obviously collected over decades. There were two chairs with silver legs topped with plastic seats tucked underneath it. Marshall pulled out the chair that had fewer things on it: a small wooden box, a coffee mug with the image of a rooster on it, and a five-pointed metal star about the size of his open hand, which he could not deduce the use of. He carefully placed these objects on the already perilous pile on top of the table and then sat down. A few moments later, Mrs. Johnson brought over a cup of almost clear tea.

"Sorry, it's not very strong. I only had a few leaves left."

"That's okay, Mrs. Johnson. This is perfect. Thank you," Marshall responded with a sympathetic smile.

Mrs. Johnson shuffled back to the kitchen, picked up a mug of tea for herself, and traversed her way to the open armchair in the living room, settling into it like a brooding hen on a clutch of eggs.

"I don't remember the last time I had company!" She said, as much to herself as to Marshall. She suddenly perked her head up and looked around the room. "Oh my, the mess!" She exclaimed as if noticing it for the first time. "Oh Marshall, I'm sorry. This place is not in a state for guests. I should never have invited you in with the place looking like this!"

"It's okay, Mrs. Johnson. My place is just as messy," he lied.

"Really?"

"Really, Mrs. Johnson. Who has time to clean these days?"

"Oh, I suppose you're right. You're a sweet boy, Marshall."

The two paused and both took a sip of tea, leaving the room in awkward silence for a moment, as neither knew what to say next.

Finally, Marshall broke the quiet. "How long have you lived here, Mrs. Johnson?"

"As long as I can remember. Although I can't remember that long. I guess my memory isn't what it once was."

Marshall suddenly was flooded with anxiety and discomfort, as if his body was shrinking within itself like a nesting doll. He regretted offering to walk Mrs. Johnson to her apartment and yearned to find a way out of this awkward interaction. He wanted to be back upstairs alone in his own apartment. In a matter of seconds, a dozen excuses to leave popped into his head, from having left the stove on or the water running, to expecting an important phone call. He took another sip of the hot, mostly flavorless tea and tried to regain control of his body by taking two deep breaths.

Once again, Marshall heard his own voice slip out of his mouth unexpectedly. "What are you waiting for, Mrs. Johnson, when you wait by the mailboxes?"

He sat there for several moments in silence, not fully sure what caused him to ask this question that he had always wondered. As the quiet seconds ticked by, Marshall first began to wonder if Mrs. Johnson had heard him at all, and wished in part that she had not. After about twenty seconds, Marshall began wondering if he had actually asked the question at all, or had the question stayed within the confines of his mind and his ears simply confused his own thoughts with actual sound.

"The mailboxes," Mrs. Johnson finally repeated in a quiet voice that was laced with doubt and sorrow. She stared into her mug as if looking for the answers in the sparse tea leaves that had settled at the bottom of it. Marshall waited as Mrs. Johnson tried to untangle the knot of memories lost and twisted by time, despair, and self-preservation.

"I...I used to get letters. I used to get letters, I think. Someone used to send me letters." Her hands began to shake, and Marshall was worried she would spill her tea. He put his own mug down, walked over to her, and gently placed his hand on hers to steady them. She looked up into his face, and he could see tears forming at the edges of her eyes. "My daughter. She...she used to send me letters. They took her from me, Marshall," she whispered it so softly he barely made out the words. "My daughter. They took her from me. They erased her," she whispered again.

As he looked into the well of grief in Mrs. Johnson's grey blue eyes, Marshall was suddenly struck with a wave of shame induced nausea. *They is me. I am they. She's talking about me.* The stifling air became overwhelming. At that moment, Marshall realized that Mrs. Johnson was the first person he had encountered whom he was certain had had a loved one erased. And with that realization, he also discovered that this was why he was alone, why he was so terrified of interacting with others. Fear of this exact moment when someone else's tragedy would hold a mirror to his own face that he could not ignore. He had been avoiding this for as long as he could remember. Now, in this poorly lit, dank smelling, shamble of an apartment, he had to finally face the only contribution he had made to society in his entire life.

"I...I'm sorry Mrs. Johnson." He looked down and saw his own hands beginning to shake and quickly let go of hers. When his gaze shifted back to her, Mrs. Johnson was once again looking into her mug. Her lips were moving ever so slightly, but he could not hear anything emanating from them. "Mrs. Johnson, I...I have to go...I..." Marshall trailed off. Mrs. Johnson sat quietly, unmoving, and it quickly became clear to Marshall that she could not hear him, that in that moment they no longer occupied the same reality. He slowly took one step back, and then another. She did not respond or move, and instead sat as still as a mannequin, unaware of his presence.

Marshall turned, made his way out of the apartment, ran up the stairs to his own and into his bathroom where he leaned over the toilet and emptied the remains of the last three standard ration meals he had eaten into the porcelain bowl.

8

March 2nd, 2084

I always felt there was something wrong with this world and today I realized that that thing that is wrong is me. Or at least I'm a part of it. Perhaps I always knew. Maybe just knowing there is something wrong, something evil, and not doing anything about it is enough. Complacency. Complicity. But I wasn't just complacent and I wasn't just complicit. I've been actively helping them. I knew all along that the "good" they convinced me I was doing was a lie. But it was easier to just go along with it, to avoid the truth, than to admit to myself that all along I've been wrong. All along I believed their lies not because they made sense, but because I wanted to. Easier than fighting it, anyway.

Marshall's hands still shook and the reek of bile hung in the air like an unwelcome fog. Vomiting left him weak and exhausted, as if he'd been wrung out like a wet towel. Yet he sat on the toilet, typing out his thoughts as best as he could.

Does that make me a coward? Too cowardly to face the truth. Too cowardly to face myself. Too cowardly to admit I've been wrong or even ask myself the question. It's so easy to just go on day after day, doing my job, coming home, eating my food, going to sleep, like a robot. Rinse and repeat. Work, refuel, work, refuel. I know Eric told me to go back in the rest of the week, pretend like nothing has happened. But how can I? How can I go back and erase more people. Maybe I erased Mrs. Johnson's daughter. How could I ever know? I wouldn't.

I don't think I can go back. They'll find me, and they'll erase me. Maybe that's for the best. We're all dead anyway, isn't that what Eric said? Maybe I'd rather be dead than keep helping them.

Marshall put the phone away. He dared not stay on it for too long. He took a shower, allowing the barely warm water to rinse off the sweat, grime, and shame of the day. He opened his mouth wide so the water could flush out his mouth, which still tasted mildly of his own sickness. And then he began to weep uncontrollably. His chest heaved as his lungs desperately attempted to refill themselves through each sob. Tears salty with regret, loss, and anger burst from his eyes, mingling with the shower water and flowing down the drain. He braced himself with an outstretched arm against the slick tiled wall as his body convulsed with the release of decades of unacknowledged sorrow and rage. In the back of his mind, Marshall knew that his phone, sitting on his bedside table, could probably hear his wails, but he did not care.

Slowly, after several minutes, his breathing began evening out and his head began to clear. He continued to feel an incredible pressure in the middle of his sternum, as if an immeasurable force was simultaneously attempting to burrow into his heart and burst out of his chest. Yet Marshall also felt as if an incredible burden had been suddenly lifted off of him. For almost his entire life, Marshall lived in darkness, under an avalanche of lies from without and repressed thoughts and feelings from within. For the first time there seemed to be light breaking through.

He turned off the water, stepped out of the shower, dried himself off, and laid down in bed. His body, normally tense as a guitar string, felt loose and at ease. Weariness quickly swallowed him into a soft embrace.

That night, Marshall slept more soundly, more peacefully than he had in almost thirty years.

9

Marshall's dreams that night were as vivid and jolting as a flash of lightning in an inky night sky. He found himself on a beach standing by the water, wearing khakis and a white button up shirt as if he were about to go to work. The sounds of the waves surrounded him and the warm sun gently caressed his face. He could feel the ocean water pouring into his shoes with every wave. Marshall noted that this should have been an uncomfortable feeling, yet his soggy shoes and socks did not bother him and he stayed standing there, slowly sinking into the sand with each passing wave.

He was surrounded by fellow beach goers in bathing suits laying out in the sun. Children were frolicking in the warm water and their laughter tickled his ears. He saw a mother in a dark red one piece bathing suit and a done up bun run up frantically to a child of about three who had been bowled over by a rogue wave, only to find him laughing and uninjured. She quickly sat down at the edge of the water and joined in with his laughter. Despite the beauty of the beach, Marshall felt completely numb to his surroundings. The joy of those around him crashed upon him like the waves in front of him, but unlike the incoming tide filling his shoes, they made no headway into his soul.

As he looked out over the water he could see the dark blue of the vast ocean meeting the periwinkle blue of the endless sky off in the distant horizon. Then the dark blue began to rise, slowly at first and then faster and faster. He realized the ocean was rising. A wave, stories tall, rushed toward the beach. Marshall began frantically trying to run but discovered his feet had sunk too far into the sand. He had stayed too long. Looking around, Marshall saw that no one else had noticed the wave, and were continuing with their day oblivious to the imminent danger rushing towards them. He yelled out, pointing at the incoming tsunami, yet no one paid him any notice.

Then the wave was upon them all. Somehow, Marshall was simultaneously in the wave and above it. Marshall watched in horror as everyone around him was swept away, unaware of what was happening. At the same time he was also being thrown around like a rag in a washing machine, completely at the whim of the currents raging around him. A few seconds later he was pulled below the water. He struggled to swim towards the surface, his lungs burning from lack of oxygen, but the wave held him down, as if the water itself was made up of countless tentacles grasping at his limbs.

Suddenly he was above the water. The beach was gone and Marshall looked up at a cliff whose ledge was both a thousand feet tall and just within his grasp at the same time. The water formed a whirlpool and pulled him in circles as he tried to make his way towards the cliff. When he was just a few feet away, he noticed the woman with black curly hair standing on the cliff, looking down at him. She wore a flowing green dress that danced in the wind. She kneeled down and reached for him, trying to bring him up to safety. He swam with the last ounces of strength he could summon and reached out to her, brushing her fingertips ever so slightly but unable to get a firm hold of her hand. With one last effort he stretched his hand out to her and grasped her hand as she grasped his. Relief flooded his system as he instantly felt safe with his hand in hers. And then the torrent pulled him back into the maelstrom and her along with him. She screamed as she plunged into the vortex.

Marshall grasped her hand knowing in the depths of his being that if he lost his grip on her they would both perish. A moment later she was swept away. He tried to open his eyes to see where she went but the salt water burned the second it came in contact with his pupils.

Within himself raged a battle between his lungs, yearning to breathe in oxygen, and his mind, knowing there was none to be had under the water. He struggled to swim towards the surface but was no longer sure which way was up. Marshall's eyes burned as he tried frantically to find the light of the sun through the water, but he was surrounded by darkness. The instinct to draw breath overwhelmed him and he closed his eyes and opened his mouth searching for the nonexistent air.

Water hurriedly dived into the open cavity, filling his throat and lungs. Marshall felt a coolness fill his chest as his lungs seized.

A loud chiming began to echo in the recesses of his mind. He opened his eyes and he was sitting in a dark stone cave that was cool and musty. His arms were tied to a chair so he could not move. A light from a fire emanated from behind him. In front of him he could see shadows projected on the cave wall in the shape of people moving to and fro, as if they were part of a puppet show. Marshall struggled against the binds, but they held him tightly. The chiming sound grew louder and louder. He screamed for help, looking around to see if anyone was there. The shadows suddenly disappeared and the woman with the black curly hair came out of the recesses of the darkness, moving as if floating above the ground. She smiled at Marshall and the panic he felt from being bound dissipated. She knelt beside him and undid the bindings, releasing him from his imprisonment, and then she stood up.

Marshall got up from the chair and turned behind him to see the large fire blazing at the back of the cave and an enormous fox with beady eyes and an evil grin holding wooden cut outs of the figures that were casting the shadows in front of him. He looked back at the woman with black curly hair and saw that she was a giant, several feet taller than him as he looked up at her. He then looked down at his hands and saw that they were the hands of a child. She was not a giant after all, but he was a toddler, much smaller than her. She held out her hand and he grasped it eagerly. The woman turned and led him down a stone hallway. Up ahead he could see a light that grew brighter and larger with each step. As they progressed up the hallway the chiming sound grew louder and louder until they reached the mouth of the cave.

Upon stepping out of the cave, the light from the sun was overwhelming, and Marshall immediately shielded his eyes from the sky, waiting for his pupils to adjust.

"Marshall," the woman said in a silky voice that filled Marshall with a deep sense of safety through the core of his being. The chiming sound grew louder, boring into his ear like a drill.

* * *

Marshall woke up to the sound of his phone ringing. It was almost 8:00 in the morning and he was already late for work.

He picked up the phone and before he could say anything a gruff, baritone voice accosted him through the phone. "MARSHALL!" Noel Reeve's voice barked, "Where the fuck are you?"

"I...I'm not feeling well this morning, Mr. Reeve," Marshall managed to reply.

"You're supposed to call in by seven o'clock when you're not coming in. You know that. You'll be docked the rest of this week's pay. Go to the doctor you're assigned to. I expect a note from him by ten o'clock."

Noel Reeve hung up the phone before Marshall could respond.

Marshall slowly rose from his bed and stretched his arms up to the ceiling, like a flower greeting the morning sun. He took a deep breath, feeling life fill his lungs. His assigned doctor was about a half mile walk from his house, but he had no intention of making that trek. Marshall became acutely aware of his own calmness. He had never been late or missed a single day of work in his entire life and was surprised at the fact that he did not feel panicked. It was also curious that his body did not react viscerally to the sounds of Noel Reeve's voice, as he usually felt queasy at the very mention of the man's name.

Until that day, March 3rd, 2084, Marshall's life took place mostly within the confines of his apartment, at the Agency of Historical Accuracy, and at the Church of the Holy American President. Rarely did he go anywhere else. Everything he needed, from toiletries to daily food rations were delivered to him weekly. He had always lived a solitary life and had no one to meet at restaurants or bars. His self-isolation was wrapped in the guise of safety and self-preservation. People were unpredictable, and everywhere else there were people. All his life, Marshall had hid behind the comfort of predictability.

Yet, it was that very predictability that was now uncomfortable. Marshall believed Eric's story was true. At the very least, he wanted to believe it, not on the merits of the story itself, but because of the story he knew, the story he had been taught all his life, had never felt right. The safe, solitary, steady life Marshall had led fit in a glass bowl cloaked by that story. Now that that cloak was removed, Marshall could begin to make out the distorted truth beyond the glass. He wanted out of the bowl.

After getting dressed, Marshal decided to do as Eric suggested, and began walking towards The Market, a gargantuan fifty-eight story building constructed of glass, steel, opulence, and taxpayer dollars. The Market towered above the Washington DC skyline like an unnaturally long finger extended over the knuckles of a closed fist. Sixteen city blocks were demolished to make way for the project, which finished just in time for the 2066 celebration of the fiftieth anniversary of the Holy American President's rise to power and subsequent saving of the country from utter ruin. The top twelve floors of The Market made up the living quarters for the Holy American President and his family. The White House had been converted to a public museum shortly after The Market was completed.

In addition to housing the Holy American President, The Market was the center of lavish commerce in the United States. Complete with an exclusive three hundred room luxury hotel, two casinos, dozens of restaurants, and stores that sold exotic and rare items that could not be acquired anywhere else in the country, The Market was the Holy American President's beacon on a hill. While the government's official stance was that The Market was open to the public, those that were not at least in the billionaire class rarely crossed the golden threshold marked by its sparkling crystal doors. For one, it would be impossible for the average citizen to buy so much as a bottle of water, for even the water in The Market was imported from the naturally filtered waterfalls of far-off lands and thus unaffordable to most. But more importantly, and intimidatingly, HALE patrolled The

Market to make sure the upper class of society were not bothered by the unsavory poor. As such, Marshall had never even dreamed of stepping foot in the building.

The Market was about a twenty-minute walk past Harmony Heights and Elmwood Estates, two neighborhoods built by Frederick Building Corp. Sparkling clean wooden signs painted with the words "Frederick Management" were attached to the dirty, worn, neglected brick facade of each tenement house. Marshall never walked through these sectors, as it was well known that the laborer class, although lauded for their patriotic commitment to keeping the country strong on the backs of their own toil, did not look kindly on government workers. But today, Marshall did not care. His sense of fear and caution had been overcome by disillusionment.

A few blocks into Harmony Heights, however, Marshall quickly began to feel the weight of his own conspicuousness. There were unwritten rules of who could go where, solely based on the measure of melanin lurking within one's skin. Marshall's melanin count was far too low to be in Harmony Heights. Like a whisper in a silent room, Marshall quickly realized he had broken into an area he did not belong in, and by doing so had tore at the fabric of the neighborhood. The faint smell of sewage and stale sweat permeated through the air. Trash littered the streets. An old, stained mattress lay in the shadow of one of the buildings. Two children of no more than six, wearing tattered T-shirts, sat on the mattress playing with a partially inflated ball. Their brown faces stared up at Marshall as he walked by. Marshall attempted a half-hearted smile, but when he did not receive any response beyond their glowering gaze, he turned his head forward and kept walking.

He passed several groups of men, all significantly larger than him, in the denim overalls of a laborer, sitting on folding chairs and talking by the sidewalk while guzzling cheap beers. He saw women hanging laundry outside of their windows and chasing children around the streets. Each time someone saw him approaching, voices would silence, legs stopped running, and arms dropped to their sides as everyone glared at him quietly. Marshall felt the unfiltered, seething hatred that could only be so openly displayed when one was outnumbered a thousand to one. He quickly took out his cellphone and held it lightly in his hand so it would be easily visible, a sign that although there was no one with him, someone, somewhere was listening.

"That ain't gonna save your skinny ass round here, white shirt." A woman of about thirty-five in a flowing maroon dress began walking up to Marshall from behind. Marshall turned his head slightly to face her but kept walking down the street. Like a summer meadow, she was plain at first glance, but after a longer look, Marshall could see true beauty, slightly dulled by the years that have worn on her. She had a long, slender face, dark soulful eyes, and skin the color of burnished copper. Marshall somehow intuited a kindness behind the scowl that she was wielding at him like a knife.

"I'm not sure what you mean," Marshall responded.

She pointed at his phone. "I saw you take that out, like that shit'll protect you. You think 'cause you got that, you're fuckin' safe? They might be listening, they might not. But they don't even come pick up the fuckin' trash 'round here. Think they're gonna barge in to save the ugly ass likes of you?"

"I...I don't want any trouble. I'm just trying to get to The Market," Marshall's pace quickened as he began to notice some of the men standing up from their folding chairs.

"If you're tryin' to hurry outta here, you're goin' the wrong fuckin' way, white shirt. Longer through than back, ya hear? Why you tryin' to get to The Market anyway? You know they ain't never lettin' your poor ass in."

"It's a public building. Anyone can go there," Marshall said, but his feet knew before his brain that she was right, and he began to slow down.

"You even stupider than you fuckin' look, white shirt. I'm guessin' you disappear and they won't even miss you. Got another white shirt ready to sit in your fuckin' seat tomorrow." By now there were several large men starting to walk over to them. Marshall stopped walking altogether. He could see there was nowhere to go.

I've been careful every single second of my life, he thought. *One stupid, impulsive moment and now I'm dead. She's right. No one will miss me. Maybe Eric. Maybe.*

Children began running over to see what was happening.

"I...I really don't want any trouble. I'll...I'll go. I should be getting home. This...this was a mistake...I..."

"Mistake is fuckin' right, white shirt. You shouldn't never have fuckin' come in here. We don't come into your clean as a whistle ***white*** shirt neighborhood. Why you comin' into ours?" Her voice dripped with malice when the word "white" slipped through her lips.

"You're...you're right. I...I shouldn't have come through here...I..." Marshall was fully surrounded now by a pack of men who towered over him like trees in a forest. Marshall began to feel himself shrinking into the ground.

"You know what we havin' tonight boy? Some fuckin' white shirt for dinner. What you say, fellas?"

"White shit more like it," came a heavy voice from the crowd. Marshall shrank a little more. He could think of no words to utter. There was no escape. He hoped beyond hope that Skeyelink was listening, that the sounds of sirens would suddenly burst through the suffocating air that surrounded him. For once, he prayed for HALE officers to come. He wished they would tear through the hoard. At that moment, he did not care how many were hurt or killed, so long as he made it back to his apartment in one piece.

"White shit," the woman continued. "I like that. You a little white shit, ain't you?"

"I...I...Please..."

"I...I...You got a bad stutter, white shit." She was now standing no more than three feet from him,

"That's enough, Marlene. Can't you see you almost got this poor boy pissing his pants?" A frail but kind voice emerged from the crowd. A second later the crowd parted and an older woman with white hair, tied in a bun, and skin of polished mahogany, slipped feebly through the hulking mass of muscles. She held a cane in one hand but seemed to walk fine without it. Her face, slightly wrinkled, reflected years of pain and hardship, but her eyes were bright and alive.

"Just having some fun, mother," the woman in the maroon dress, who was apparently named Marlene, smiled at Marshall. The men around him suddenly broke out in raucous laughter and began dispersing back to their folding chairs, dragging the children with them. "Just messing with you, white shirt. What did you think? Did you think we were going to murder you and bury you in the backyard? Chop you up and throw you into tonight's stew? You think we're out here eating our pets and we might eat you too?" She laughed a laugh that was founded in rage and sadness. Marshall noticed the cadence of her speech was suddenly different.

"I...uh..."

"No hard feelings, white shirt. You don't know any better. We're not the animals they say we are. All things being equal though, you're not too bright strolling in here like you own the place." With that, Marlene blew him a kiss, turned on her heels and sauntered off in the direction she came from.

"Don't mind my daughter, son. She's spunky but she wouldn't harm a fly, much less the likes of you. You're really heading to The Market?"

"Ye..ye..yes," Marshall stammered, his body still wracked with terror as his mind tried to comprehend his sudden reversal of fortunes. A fleeting moment prior he was contemplating imminent pain and eventual death, and all of a sudden he was speaking to a seemingly kindly old woman about his travel plans.

"My daughter's right, you know. They're never letting you in there. Why are you heading there anyway?"

"I...I don't know. I..I just...it's been a strange week."

"It's only Wednesday, son. You got a long week ahead of you."

"Right...it's been a strange couple of days. I just..I don't know. I just started walking that way. Made sense at the time."

"It made sense at the time? Made sense to walk your white shirt through Harmony Heights to a place that you can't get into? Doesn't make a whole lot of sense to me, son. What's your name, anyway?"

"Marshall."

"Marshall? Marshall. I'm Coretta. You've obviously met my daughter, Marlene." She held out her hand and Marshall shook it lightly.

"Thank you."

"Thank me for what?"

"For...for saving me."

"You weren't in any danger for me to save you from, son. Come, sit. Have a beer with us. Least I could do after Marlene's antics."

"I...I really should be going," Marshall suddenly realized he was still holding his phone in his hand, and slowly put his phone back into his pocket.

"Nonsense. You were on your way to get kicked out of The Market. Now that that ingenious plan has been thoroughly derailed, you have plenty of time for a beer. I insist. Come have a seat."

Marshall hesitated. This whole morning has been out of the ordinary. He had veered completely off track and it was only a matter of time before Skeyelink flagged his behaviors and he would have to offer an explanation that he did not have. Going home would be the safe choice. Or making his way to the doctors and feigning some sort of illness. It would be the choice he had always made. *We're all dead already.*

"Okay. Sure. One beer"

"Excellent. Come, right this way." She led him over to the small front yard of one of the brick buildings. There were three black metal folding chairs sitting on a dirt lawn spotted with intermittent tufts of grass and clover. As she walked over she waved over to a group of men one building over and showed them four fingers. A moment later, a tall man with a smooth shaved head, a thin mustache, and deep brown skin walked over to them with four ice cold beers, two in each hand.

"Marshall, this is my nephew, Martin. Martin, this is Marshall."

Martin pinned two beers between his left arm and his torso and stuck out his right hand. Marshall shook it. Martin smirked slightly and he shook Marshall's hand vigorously with a vice-like grip. "Pleasure."

"Pleasure is mine," Marshall replied as he consciously maintained an even face while his innards twisted from the crushing strength of Martin's right hand. After what seemed to Marshall like several minutes, but was in fact only a few seconds, Martin released his hand, to Marshall's great relief, and handed him 2 cans of beer.

"Thanks," Marshall said as he clasped the beer with his left hand while he attempted to discreetly place the cold aluminum against the skin of his withered right.

"Don't mention it," Martin responded. He winked at his aunt, handed her two beers and walked back next door.

Marshall looked back at Coretta, who smiled at him. "Strong boy, he is. Very protective of me. Sorry about your hand. Come, have a seat." Coretta sat in the chair on the left, placed a beer on the ground next to her, carefully making sure it was shaded by the chair, and cracked open the other. Marshall sat in the chair on the right, leaving a chair between them. The chairs were angled in slightly. Marshall tried to get comfortable on the hard metal. He could feel the hot sun bearing down like a bloodshot eye staring at him. Coretta did not seem to notice the heat.

"Better start on that beer before it's warm as soup," she nodded to Marshall's can, which was still unopened in his hands. Alcohol was a luxury that Marshall rarely felt he could afford. Nor did he enjoy the effects of it. The idea of losing control of one's inhibitions was a terrifying idea. People have been erased for saying or doing the wrong things while drunk.

We're all dead already.

Marshall opened the beer and took a sip. The cold liquid, crisp and bitter, flowed down his throat. He took a deep breath through his nose and felt the fear and apprehension slowly beginning to dissolve.

"It's not the best. But it'll get the job done. So, tell me, Marshall. What are you really doing here?"

"I was heading to The..."

"Yes, yes, you were going to The Market. But I don't think you're stupid enough to think you were actually getting in there. So, I ask again. What are you doing here? Shouldn't you be at work anyway? Working for the HAP?"

"I guess I don't know, exactly. I was just...I realized something this morning and I just started walking. That's the best I can explain it really." Marshall paused for a moment, looking for a way to deflect the conversation away from himself. "How about them? How come you're all drinking beers in the middle of the morning? It's only ten o'clock! Shouldn't they be at work too?" Marshall nodded in the direction of Martin.

"Everyone here works nightshifts. Right now is our five o'clock in the afternoon," she said dismissively. "But don't change the subject. What did you realize?"

Marshall glanced at his phone, hidden in his pants, and then took a long sip of his beer, trying to give himself time to think about how to answer that question, since he knew the truth was not an option.

"You're thinking about what lies to tell me. That's okay. I understand. You're worried about that spy in your pocket."

"I wasn't, I..."

"Now you're lying about the lies you were thinking about. Marshall, they don't even need to listen in on you. I bet you've never stepped a toe out of line your whole life, with or without that phone. And yet here you are, walking through a black neighborhood towards the president's castle. You lose your mind in the last couple hours?"

Marshall sat silently for a moment. The condensation coming off the can of beer slowly dripped over his hands. *Have I lost my mind? Doesn't feel that way.* Marshall closed his eyes and took another deep breath. Even though the air he was filling his lungs with was swampy and hot, tinted with the odor of rubbish and hard labor, Marshall felt refreshed by it. In that moment he could feel several things at once. He felt the rhythmic muscular machinery of his heart beating in his chest. He felt the pulsating throbs of his blood flowing through his hands and feet.. He felt the heat of the sun on his forehead and the beads of sweat dripping down his face. And he felt a clarity of mind and self-awareness that was wholly foreign to him. *I actually feel better, more sane right now than I ever have. Maybe this is what insanity feels like.*

"Maybe," he replied. "Maybe I have." And he smiled at Coretta over his beer.

She smiled back. "Well then it seems like insanity suits you, Marshall. That's a good name, by the way. Where'd you get that name? I'm assuming you're not named after Thurgood."

"Who?"

"Thurgood Marshall? Ah, not surprised you don't know him. He's been erased from history, or at least from written history. Only way to keep him alive is to talk about him."

"No, no I've never heard of him. I don't know where I got my name. No one was around to tell me."

"Oh, I see. Sorry to hear that, son. But whoever gave you that name, they chose a good one. A solid one."

"How about your name? Coretta. Never heard that name before.

"Named after Coretta Scott King."

"Never heard of her either..."

"She was a writer, an activist. She fought for civil rights. And Martin Luther King was her husband." Marshall stared at her blankly. "Never heard of him either huh?" Marshall shook his head. "Figures. There was a time he had his own holiday, you know. But those days are long past us. This country is great again for folks like you. But us? For us, we went back a hundred years."

"I'm not sure what you're talking about. I didn't learn anything about this in school."

"School! HA! You didn't go to school, Marshall. School's a place that teaches you how to think for yourself. School's a place that gives you the knowledge you need to make good decisions. You didn't go to school, Marshall. There hasn't been a school in this country since I was a child. No, what you went to was a conditioning program. They told you everything you needed to know to be a good little citizen. They taught you that they were the good guys, that everyone else was the bad guys, and then they set you on your way to live a life of servitude."

"Servitude?"

"Yes, Marshall. Servitude. You're a slave, you just get paid for it."

"Well, how about your kids? How about...about, Marlene? Did she learn something different?"

"Of course she did. Just not in one of your programs."

"Your kids go to different scho...I mean, programs?"

"You think our kids get an education? We are laborers, Marshall. Our patriotic duty is to labor. Don't need an education for that. But I'll tell you this. We know more than any one graduating from one of your programs."

"So, you teach your kids yourselves"

"Of course we do. Hard to teach without any books or supplies but we manage. And at least they know truth from lies."

Marshall began to wonder if she knew the same story that Eric told him just a few days ago. He was about to ask when he remembered the voice box, and all the precautions Eric put in place, and the phone in his pocket.

This conversation has gone too far, Marshall thought as his right hand subconsciously drifted toward his pocket. He drank the rest of his beer and stood up.

"I should probably get going."

"Already?"

"I've probably already stayed too long. I...I'm supposed to go to the doctor's you see. I...Thank you. Thanks for the beer and the, uh...education."

"Anytime, Marshall. Thanks for wandering into our neck of the woods." She bent over, grabbed her second beer, stood up slowly and offered her hand, which Marshall shook warmly. She handed him the beer. "For the road."

"Uh, thanks," Marshall responded, as he accepted the beer and slipped it into his pocket, immediately feeling awkward at the obvious bulge of the can.

"Walk safely, Marshall, and stay out of trouble. I hope our paths cross again, so til next time."

"Um...sure. Til next time," Marshall responded, even though he could not fathom how their paths would ever cross in the future.

10

Oftentimes in dreams, dreamers find themselves in spots that their mind identifies as a specific and familiar place, yet the dreamer's eyes acknowledge it looks nothing like said location. To Marshall, the walk back to Prospera Haven felt eerily like one of those dreams. His mind knew this was Washington DC. It was the same city he had lived in his entire life, the same asphalt streets and concrete sidewalks, and the same uniform brick buildings lining those sidewalks. The heat was still stifling and like most days, the air hung thick around him like wet laundry. Yet somehow everything he saw looked unfamiliar in one way or another.

Things that he must have seen thousands of times, that he had walked by and glossed over every day and had faded into the background of monotony suddenly became crisp and novel. He noticed the potholes that peppered the streets and the lightning shaped cracks in the sidewalks that his feet automatically danced around through decades of repetition and practice. He noticed the street signs that hung at almost every intersection were dented, bent, or missing altogether. The trees that lined the road were withered and bare or had been cut down and left as stumps to remind everyone of what once stood in its place. Upon noticing the naked limbs of the cherry blossom trees, Marshall immediately recognized the lack of greenery around him. The city was a cornucopia of stone and metal, dust and ash.

Most of all, Marshall noticed the people. At this time of day, he was normally at work and was not privy to the comings and goings of the people that wandered the streets during the middle of the day. The fact that there were far more women walking around than men at first startled Marshall, but quickly he realized this made sense. Since women were only allowed specific jobs, such as librarians, school teachers, secretaries, and stewardesses, the majority of women were unemployed homemakers who were preparing the evening meals by the time he got out of work each day and were therefore safely tucked away in their own homes when Marshall was generally outside.

As he walked home, he passed dozens of women pushing strollers, carrying shopping bags, and sitting by the one playground he passed watching their children play on the dilapidated structures. Most were finely dressed in bright colors that popped against their alabaster skin and muted expressions. Not a single one of them so much as glanced at Marshall as he slithered his way along the crumbling sidewalks and around the other people walking.

The men he saw on his walk were few and far between. While the women moved with purpose, these men puttered along like blind fish in a strong current. This also made sense to Marshall. These men were clearly without jobs, and as such were generally shunned by society at large for their lack of masculine ingenuity. Without employment, they were not eligible for any government programs or assistance, compassion or sympathy. Labeled as "losers" and "low-IQ" with "bad genes" by the Holy American President, unemployed white men were looked upon almost as hatefully as brown skinned terrorists.

In the past, Marshall never paid any attention to these men when he passed them on the street, walking by them as if they were lamp posts or fire hydrants. That day he saw them for the first time, and noticed that unlike the women who walked by him without notice, these men stared at him. He made eye contact with many of them, at first quickly looking away, hoping they did not notice. But after a few, he began looking back at them, and saw behind their eyes a world beyond desperation.

There was one particular man, who, despite the heat, was wearing tattered jeans, a red checkered flannel shirt, and a discolored, dirt stained orange beanie that caught Marshall's attention a few blocks from his home. The man was lying in the small alley between two brick buildings, hiding from the sun and people writ large. What Marshall could see of his face behind the scraggly, unkept salt and pepper bead and mustache was covered in reddish brown spots. His forlorn grey blue eyes, which were sunken deep into the caverns of his eye sockets, stared out vacantly as if looking far into the future or far into the past.

Marshall had a thought to give the man some money, at least enough for a meal, but doubted the man had a phone to transfer money to. He felt the can of beer in his pocket, which was already warming up with the warmth of the day and the heat of his body. He pulled it out and took a step towards the man, stretching the beer out towards him.

"Sir," Marshall said meekly. "Would you like this? I'm not going to drink it."

The man made no movement. He did not blink or look up. He did not acknowledge Marshall's presence in the slightest.

"Sir?"

The man continued to stare blankly ahead.

Marshall's hand slowly retreated as he placed the beer back into his pocket. At first, Marshall thought the man was being impolite, ignoring him so blatantly. But then he noticed did not seem to be breathing. Marshall shuddered and quickly took a step back. The man continued to lie there, completely still. Several people walked by without so much as a glance at him, as Marshall stared down at him in horror. Then he turned and quickly walked away.

* * *

A while later, Marshall found himself in front of the windowed door of Blair's antiques. He was not sure how he had got there or why. The time between him walking away from the man, whom he was now sure was dead, and arriving at the antique shop seemed to have been erased from his memory, as if stolen by a thief in the night.

Marshall opened the door, hearing the familiar jingle of the bell, and looked to his left. Eric was not behind the counter. He looked over the shop, scanning the bookshelves filled with a bounty of mostly useless items, but did not see anyone.

"Be right with you!" Came Eric's cheerful voice from the back room. A moment later, Eric appeared and the smile on his face quickly faded as he saw Marshall standing next to the front door.

"Marshall! Well this is a surprise. It's Thursday! And, the middle of the day! What are you doing here?"

"I…I don't know, to be honest."

"Come, come, let's go in the back. I just put on a pot of coffee."

Eric led Marshall to the back room, where they did the now familiar dance of taking out their phones and the voice box and then quietly sneaking out the back door.

Once they were securely in the room deep underground, Eric asked in a stern voice, dripping with concern, "What the hell are you doing here?"

Marshall, shaking slightly, pulled the can of beer out of his pocket, placed it on the side table between the two armchairs, and sat down. He stared quietly at his knees, trying to sort through the maze of his mind to figure out where to begin.

Eric glanced at the beer and said, "Ah, you saw Coretta today, didn't you."

Marshall looked up at him with astonishment in his eyes. "How, how do you know Coretta?"

"You think I told you to go through Harmony Heights on a whim? Figured you would go after work or on Sunday...Not in the middle of a weekday. So you couldn't go back to work, huh? Couldn't stomach erasing the memory of people anymore?"

Marshall explained about Mrs. Johnson.

"Okay, I don't blame you. I get it. But you coming here in the middle of the day, when you're supposed to be at work, that was a mistake. We're going to have to speed things up a bit now."

"Speed things up? Speed what up?"

"Well, it's time for you to say goodbye to everything you've ever known. You join The Resistance today. It's that, or good chance you're going to get erased in the next couple days."

"I..I don't have a choice now do I?"

"No, you don't. It'll take a few days. Any red flags picked up by Skeyelink have to be screened by HALE. They only have so many people reviewing these red flags and my guess is you're low on the priority list. You've never stepped a toe out of line your entire life. They've got thousands of red flags to get through before they get to you. But they will. It's just a matter of time. So it's time for you to go."

"Go where? What do I do? Where do I go?"

"Take a breath, Marshall. You're going to be okay. We'll wait a bit until it's dark and then I'll send you on your way."

"On my way where?"

"Somewhere safe. You've been working for the wrong side all your life, Marshall. It's time we changed that."

Marshall sat silently for several minutes. His mind sat with him, quiet. He tried to will thoughts, a reaction, into being, but could only think about his lack of one. *This is all too much,* was the only thought that fully formed and echoed back and forth within the recesses of his skull, like a drop of water hitting a pool in a dark and empty cavern. Suddenly he felt extremely parched.

"Ca...ca...can I have something to drink?"

"Of course. I'll be right back."

Eric grabbed the beer off of the table and went through the door at the back of the room, through which Marshall had never been, and left him alone with his thoughts, or lack there of, and the art on the walls. Marshall had a momentary instinct to run.

Perhaps if I leave now, grab my phone, and go to work, I can explain everything. Mr. Reeve will understand. Then I can just go back to my life and everything will be fine. Like I never walked into this place.

But at the exact same moment Marshall knew that was not a choice he could make. There was no chance they would let him return to his previous life. And there was no chance they would let Eric live either. That was not something Marshall could stomach. He knew he had done enough damage, erased enough people in his life. He could not be the one to bring Eric down as well.

Eric stepped back through the door with a tray that held two glasses and two decanters, one of apple juice and one of water. He set the tray on the table between the two chairs, sat down, and poured himself some apple juice.

"This is my favorite. Apple juice always quenches my thirst the best," he commented.

Marshall followed suit and poured himself a glass and took a sip. The aroma of the juice instantly revived his senses as he brought it to his lips, and the sweetness as it flowed over his tongue rejuvenated his mind. He put the glass down and took a deep breath, filling his lungs to capacity, and then released it back into the room. He looked over at Eric, who wore the same, kindly smile he remembered from the very first time he walked into the antique shop. A rush of memories from the past few months streamed through his mind, not as individual scenes or conversations, but as a general feeling, like a mosaic of all the Tuesdays he spent with Eric, coalescing into one larger picture. In that moment, he felt absolute trust in this man sitting opposite him. He knew that he could place his life in Eric's hands and that everything would turn out for the best.

"So what do we do now?"

"Same thing we always do, Marshall. We talk. We have some time to kill before it gets dark. You must have a million questions. I'll answer what I can."

Marshall thought for a moment.

"How do you know Coretta?" Was the first question that popped into Marshall's mind.

"Well we met about forty years ago. Been married for thirty-seven. I'm assuming you met our daughter, Marlene?"

"What? Married! How can you be married?"

"Well we married in secret. We see each other when we can, never in public of course."

"I...I don't understand."

"There was a time in this country when anyone could marry anyone. White could marry black, men could marry men, women could marry women."

"Men? Marry other men? Women other women? Why would they do that?" Marshall's face revealed his inner shock.

"Because they loved each other, Marshall. Homosexuality isn't a disease to be cured, no matter how much the president says it is. And he didn't cure it, by the way. There are still gay people in this country, they're just no longer able to be who they are in public."

"I...I don't know...I've never met one."

"I bet you have, you just don't know it. But back to our story. You know, this country made incredible advances during the second half of the twentieth century. One was civil rights, pushing for all people, regardless of skin color, to have the same rights and opportunities. That included the opportunity to marry who you wanted. But this president reversed all the advancements our country made. Slowly but surely he made this country hate again. At the time I met Coretta, interracial marriage was still technically legal, but clearly looked down upon. And when the president looked down on something, he made it clear that anyone who disagreed would be punished, even if it wasn't illegal."

"Punished how?"

"Well, he started with companies, law firms, universities that he didn't like. He punished them by taking away federal funding, refusing to allow them to interact with the federal government, canceling federal grants, basically using the power of the government for his own personal revenge. One by one, most of these companies fell in line. Remember what I said before? Money is power? He discovered that the federal government has the most money, and he could wield that money like a sledgehammer to force people into submission. When I met Coretta, gay marriage had already been made illegal again and it was already clear that interracial marriages were not going to be tolerated much longer. He said in no uncertain terms that churches or institutions that did not follow his moral code would lose their nonprofit status, and be subjected to incredibly high taxes and fines. Unsurprisingly, the churches all caved. And this is why we had to marry in secret. It's a marriage just between us and the people who know us."

"So do you live together? How does that work?"

"We see each other when we can, mostly underground. You'll understand that soon enough. There's a whole world out there you don't know about."

Marshall sat for a moment, mulling over the picture Eric just painted of an America where people could marry whomever they wanted. It did not seem plausible. From everything Marshall had been taught, homosexuality was a disease that had infected the country and was destroying families, but had thankfully been eradicated, and the mixing of the races was an abomination. He knew this was not a thought he would easily be able to rewire, so he decided to change the subject.

"Tell me about The Resistance. What is it?"

"People who believe that there's a better country, a better world to be had. People who know the truth and are willing to fight and die so that future generations can be free from the tyranny we live under today. We're in every city, everywhere across the country. But here in D.C., this is where we are centered."

"Why D.C.?"

"Well, it's the center of power. It's where the biggest fight will happen."

"Fight? How will you fight them? They have all the weapons, the guns!"

"First, they don't have all the guns. You know, when he first came to power, most of his supporters believed in this thing called the second amendment. There were millions and millions of guns in the United States. He promised them he would make sure they kept that right. Ironically enough, many gun owners believed it was their duty to own one to defend the constitution, in case people in the government became too strong and began infringing on people's rights, and some sort of revolution was necessary. And they supported the exact person that absorbed all the power and demolished the constitution and turned this country into the exact thing it was born to fight. You see, the way authoritarians work is they always want more authority, more power, no matter how much they have. And the more power they accumulate, the more scared they are to lose it. When it started to become clear even to his followers that *his* government was the one that they had always kept their guns to defend against, he decided it was time to take away the last line of defense for American citizens. He abolished the second amendment and confiscated all the guns. Luckily by that time, The Resistance had already been born, and we were able to save enough weapons. But at the end of the day, we only have guns. We don't have armored vehicles, we don't have tanks, we don't have planes, we don't have nearly enough to defeat the United States military, which he controls."

"So then what's the point? Why are we fighting if we can't win?"

"You're right, we can't beat them by force. But force isn't the source of their power. It's not the military, it's not their guns, it's not HALE. It's Skeyelink and Facts. It's the world they've built inside your head. It's the constant stream of lies that are taken for truth. There are almost two hundred million Americans in this country. How many are part of HALE? How many are part of his government? It's a small fraction. Most are just regular citizens trying to live their lives. If we can reveal the man behind the curtain, if we can show all of America the lies they've been told and believe, then we have a chance to free this country from tyranny. Tyranny's fuel is fear and silence, Marshall. Tyranny lives on voluntary subservience. But to live under tyranny is not natural. Humans are not dogs, loyal to masters even when they abuse them. Humans do not yearn for the yoke. Our natural state is to be able to choose our own destinies, to connect with other humans, to find kinship rather than hate. All those things fly in the face of tyranny. We don't win by fighting in the streets. We win by revealing the truth, by taking down the curtain, by going after the people who fuel the lies, and by joining together. Arrogance is their greatest weakness, Marshall. They believe themselves invincible. They truly believe they are better, stronger, smarter, than the rest of us. But they're wrong. And the people outnumber them thousands to one. We just need to make the people realize who the true enemy are, who have leached the wealth from this country and left the rest of us begging for scraps off their gold-plated dinner tables. If we all decide we'll no longer live under their whips, they cannot stop us. We can return this country back to the principles it was founded on."

"What principles are those?"

"That all people are equal, that everyone has the same rights, that we can disagree without fear of retribution from the President, and that no one, citizen or not, should be erased without warning, without due process. People like the president, born rich, often believe they are better than others. They believe they deserve the wealth and power that came to them, not because they were lucky enough to be born into that situation, but because they think they're somehow superior and earned it. They'll never understand, and therefore will never truly care about the challenges of everyday people. That is why this country was founded based on a government of the people. Because those born into wealth, power, and royalty cannot empathize with the rest of us, and rarely put the needs of the people above their own. We lost those principles along the way. The rich and powerful slowly chipped away at it until we are where we are now. But tyranny is not a natural state, and the people will always break free of it sooner or later. It's just a matter of time."

"You truly believe that? That the people can rise up and win?"

"Yes. We have to. Because what other choice do we have? It's either fight or accept. We're all here for a short period of time, Marshall. I've pulled the curtain back for you. You've seen the small man manipulating the controls. Now it's time to fight."

"But what can I do?"

"Oh, we'll find a job for you. Don't you worry about that. Big things are happening, and soon."

"What things?"

"That you'll find out soon enough."

"What happens if I get caught? What happens when HALE grabs one of us?"

Eric reached out and put his hand on Marshall's, which was resting on the arm rest of his chair. "I'm not going to sugarcoat this for you. If one of us gets caught, we do what we can to not divulge any information about The Resistance. Don't worry, all of us are pretty siloed. You won't know more than you need to and definitely not enough to do permanent damage. But if you're asking if you'll be rescued? Well, no. There's no rescue, there's no saving. We do have some people on the inside and will do what we can to slip you a razor or something so you can end things on your own terms, but that's the best we can do."

"That's it? The best you can do is offer me is a razor to open up my own veins?"

"Yes. We're all dead anyway, Marshall. Remember that. The vast majority of humans who have ever lived on this planet have been forgotten, their names, who they were, what they liked to eat, the things that brought them joy, their stories, gone. Lost in the river of time, drowned by the never-ending flow of new people, new stories. Even the names who were once famous, King, Tubman, Kennedy, Obama, or infamous, like Hitler, Franco, Stalin have been purposefully erased from history by the president. The only thing that might remain is if the actions you take, the choices you make, somehow change the society that lives on after you're gone. Even if you only move it a quarter inch, that change, or the change that you're a part of, that is the only legacy one can hope to leave. Three, four generations from now, your name, my name, the specific things we did, will all be gone. No one will know. But if we can move the needle just a hair, if we can open some eyes and show people that the world can be better if we fight for it, then we will live on in that new world we helped create. Do you understand?"

Marshall nodded, not fully convinced, but also knowing he had no other choice. He took another sip of apple juice, savoring the flavor and the cool feeling the liquid brought to his throat.

After a moment, Eric broke the silence. "You must be hungry. Did you even eat breakfast?"

"Come to think of it, no, I haven't eaten anything really all day."

"Wait here, I'll bring us some sandwiches."

Eric disappeared behind the door again and a few minutes later came back out with a plate holding a turkey and cheese sandwich with lettuce and tomatoes. Marshall rarely had fresh produce and his eyes opened wide at the crisp greens and reds of the vegetables.

"Thank you," he said appreciatively as he was handed a plate. His stomach, which seemed to be dormant the entire day, woke like a sleeping giant, grumbling angrily. Marshall quickly devoured the sandwich.

Eric chuckled, "Having your entire life pulled out from under you sure does build up an appetite."

"I guess so," Marshall replied, grabbing his glass of apple juice and finishing it off.

"Be right back." Eric took the plate and the tray and took it back through the door. When he finally came out he was holding something Marshall had never seen before.

"I have a few things that need taking care of right now before you go. Here, a little education while you wait for it to get dark," Eric handed Marshall a rectangular object consisting of what appeared to be uniformly shaped leaves. "It's a book, Marshall."

Marshall's eyes went wide as he scanned the cover. "It Can't Happen Here," he read aloud.

"Oh, but it can," Eric chuckled to himself.

"Whe...where did you get this?"

"Just like the guns. Many people saw the writing on the wall, so to speak. When it was clear that the nationwide book burning was inevitable, people around the country simultaneously began hiding what they could. Over time, The Resistance has been able to amass quite the library. We have them in every city, they're just very well hidden. You see, we're not just fighting against tyranny, we're also fighting to save knowledge, art, and all the things that make life worth living. The president was intent on destroying everything that made him look bad or that he didn't understand, which, to be frank, was almost everything. He tried to take over not just the government and the military, but the entire culture of the country. And so he began destroying art, music, museums, and literature. But you can't destroy the human spirit so easily."

"You have a whole library of these things?" Marshall said in awe and shock as he marveled over the object in his hands, which felt both wondrous and daunting.

"Yup! And movies, music, all kinds of things he wanted destroyed. Maybe you'd like to see it?"

"Yes! Yes, I would love to see it."

"Then we'll make it happen."

"What's this book about? What do you mean by education?"

"It's fiction. You'll see."

"Fiction? What can I learn from something that isn't true?"

"What you'll learn soon enough is that oftentimes fiction will tell you more about reality than reality."

"I, I don't understand."

"That's okay. You will. But first, I have a few things to do. I'll be back in a bit. Enjoy the book," and Eric disappeared behind the door.

Marshall turned over the foreign object in his hands, feeling the cover against his skin. Of all the objects that could fall into Marshall's possession, the book in his hands was one of the most forbidden. Being caught with it meant instant erasure. There was a sudden energy, a vibration, that he felt emanating from beneath his sternum, as if the book itself was coursing a current of power up his arms and into his heart, which was thumping loud and clear like a drum. He ran a finger up the spine and then let the book fall open. The paper smelled of wood and dust and knowledge. At first, he was unsure how to hold it, how to turn the pages. His thumbs felt clumsy trying to grasp and turn the pages. It took him a few moments to find the first page, after the title page and copyright pages, which were unfamiliar to him. The letters themselves seemed dull against the off white paper and his eyes had to adjust to the words that were not silhouetted against the bright background of a screen. More than once he instinctively swiped the page in an attempt to turn it, forgetting that he was not holding his phone or a tablet. But after a while, he began to grasp the physical mechanics of the book, and as his fingers learned to manipulate the pages on their own, his mind began sinking into the story. Over the next three hours, Marshall eased into the world Sinclair Lewis created like slipping on a comfortable pair of slippers.

There were myriad characters Marshall got the sense that he should know or recognize. The author wrote about them as if they were household names, like Hitler, Mussolini, and Napoleon, but Marshall had not heard of any of them. Similarly, there were many words that were not in his vocabulary, like fascism and dictatorship. Despite this, Marshall quickly began seeing the parallels between what was happening in the book and the story Eric had told him about the Holy American President's rise to power. The stories mirrored each other so closely that Marshall began wondering if Eric's tale was lifted almost directly from this book.

About halfway through the novel, Eric came back into the room.

"What do you think, enjoying it?"

"I think so. I don't know if enjoying is the right word. It feels awfully dark. And to be honest, it sounds a lot like the story you told about…"

"About the Holy American President? Yes, yes it does, doesn't it. That book was written over a hundred years ago. But that story has happened several times, in different ways, in different countries. There's a blueprint to how people like the Holy American President destroy democracies and take power."

"If there's a blueprint, if people knew how it's done, then why did people let it happen?"

"Not enough people, Marshall. You see, people believe what they want to believe. More than anything, people want to believe two things: that they're better than others, and that they're right. There's a righteous comfort that comes from feeling superior. It's a blanket that the insecure cover themselves with. And the Holy American President gave people the thickest, warmest blanket you could imagine. He pointed to people who had darker skin, who were gay, who were poor, who believed in a different god, and told his supporters, 'You are better than these people. You deserve more than these people. And I am the only one who can rid you of these people.' His followers accepted the blanket and used it to cover their eyes from what was happening right in front of them. By the time they peaked out from behind it, it was already too late. But like I said, educational, right? Fiction can be a window into truth, if you only look for it."

"Can I keep this? I'd like to finish it."

"No, not right now. I can't let you leave with it. But I'll get it back to you. I promise."

"Okay," Marshall replied as he hesitantly handed the book back to Eric. "Wait, where have you been anyway? It's been hours!"

"I had some things I needed to take care of. Errands, of a sort."

Marshall looked back at the door. "Back there?"

"I'll explain later. It's time for you to go. Now listen carefully. Across the street is the start of Morris Road. You know where Stanton Road is?"

Marshall nodded vigorously, with his eyes laser focused on Eric's mouth, as if watching the words escaping from his mouth might help him etch these directions into his long term memory.

"Okay, good. Cut over to Stanton Road and follow it south, past the parkway, until you get to Carlson Rd. It's the one right after Shippen. If you hit Tanner Street you've gone too far. You're looking for 1504 Carlson."

"1504 Carlson," Marshall repeated.

"Exactly. You're going to go right up to the front door and knock three times. They'll let you in."

"And then what?"

"Then that's it. They'll tell you what to do next."

"Who?"

"People you can trust. They know all about you already."

"What? How?"

"Marshall, how do you think?" Eric asked with a slight wink.

"Oh. Right. What about my phone? Do I bring.."

"Your phone is already gone."

"What? Gone? How?"

"It's been picked up and disposed of."

Marshall's instant reaction was anger. He had had his phone his entire life, always within arms reach. Logically, he knew it was a terrible thing, an overseer he kept in his pocket that enslaved him. Yet there was solace in having it in his pocket or knowing where it was. Having it suddenly ripped from his life felt like a deep loss that he could not understand.

Eric sensed his unease. "It's okay. You're not going to need it anymore. But please, it's time to go. Here, put this on. You don't want to be wearing that white shirt out there."

Eric handed him a black cotton jacket with a hood, which Marshall promptly put on. Marshall stood up and started walking towards the door, then paused for a second and then turned around to face Eric.

"Will I see you again?"

"Marshall, my boy, I promise we'll see each other again. Probably sooner than you'd like. Now go on."

Marshall nodded. He walked upstairs, into the kitchenette where he noticed the empty table that the two of them had consumed countless coffees, both as themselves and as virtual imitations of themselves. Marshall continued through the door, through the maze of bookshelves in the antique store, and out the front door of the shop. The little bell jingled as he walked out.

11

When Marshall stepped out of the antique shop, darkness had fallen over the city like oil, thick and choking, seeping into every crack and gutter, coating the streets with silence. Not many people ventured out after dark, knowing that HALE patrolled the capital. Marshall kept to the shadows, his ears keen to hear any noise that might cut through the quiet. He went to grab his phone to check what time it was but then realized he no longer had it. As soon as his hand slipped out of his empty pocket, it dawned on him that he did not have a GPS or any way of mapping his route. Worried about losing his way, he began repeating the directions to himself over and over again, as he did his best to focus on the road ahead.

It took Marshall about thirty minutes to walk to Carlson Road. For the most part, the walk was quiet and easy. He did not see anyone else walking, nor did any cars pass by. Despite this, Marshall's nervous system was on high alert for the entire walk, and by the time he got to Carlson Road, he was drenched in sweat, and his body was shaking with anxiety.

1504 Carlson Road was a squat three story brick row house squeezed between several other homes with nearly identical footprints, but different exteriors. The numbers sat vertically on the frame of the door. The number 4 was missing but its shadow remained against the white trim. The windows were completely dark, and it did not appear as though anyone was home.

Marshall crept quietly up to it, knocked softly, and waited for several seconds. A dog barked sadly in the distance. There was no response. He placed his ear gently to the door and heard nothing. Panic began to creep in like an intruder in the dark. *Maybe I've been had,* he thought. *What if this was all a trick? Maybe none of this is real. What am I even doing here? And now I don't have my phone. I'm going to be erased for sure. Could everything Eric told me be a lie?*

A rumbling sound that could only belong to a large vehicle slowly began filtering over the rooftops from several blocks away. Marshall knew the only vehicles that might make that sound at this time of night were large military vehicles that patrolled the streets to keep the peace and ensure public safety. In effect, they kept everyone quietly tucked away in their homes. The sound made Marshall's stomach twist into a knot and his sweat soaked shirt and jacket suddenly felt cold, despite the hot March night.

Marshall frantically looked to the left and right as dread began wrapping its tentacles around his imagination. There was no way to tell if the HALE truck would turn down Carlson Road, but Marshall did not want to risk it. He then saw a doorbell on the right side of the door, which he had missed when he first walked up the stoop. He tapped it furiously, hoping he would hear the chimes of the bell behind the door, which now felt like a drawbridge between him and safety. No sound emanated from within the house, but the growling of the heavy engines grew louder. He could sense they were only a block away.

The end of the street began to brighten from the headlights of the truck. It was said that these trucks had infrared cameras and could even spot the body signatures of citizens through solid walls. Marshall was not certain this was true, but he had no intention of finding out. He banged on the door loudly three times, hoping that the sound could not be heard by the soldiers inside the truck over the rumble of its engine.

Just as the headlights became visible the door opened, a hand grabbed Marshall's shirt and pulled him into near perfect darkness. The door closed just as quickly. Marshall was dragged blindly down what he assumed to be a hall. He was then stood up roughly. A hand grabbed his hand and placed it on what felt like a wooden banister.

A hand grasped his shoulder and a soft voice whispered sternly into his ear, "downstairs, quickly."

Marshall took a cautious step down and found the first stair beneath his right foot. He grasped the banister firmly both to keep himself from falling down the stairs and to find some sort of grounding, subconsciously trying to expel the fear that had an equally firm grip on his body.

After about a dozen steps, the hand on his shoulder pulled him back, stopping him from moving forward, and then moved him to the side. He felt a body brush past him. There was the sound of metal on metal in the darkness and then a soft creaking sound of a door opening, accompanied by a woosh of cool air. Marshall was pushed forward a few more steps and heard a door close behind him.

The light that suddenly went on was blinding. It was a soft, yellow light but after the complete darkness of the stairwell, it felt like a flashlight had just been shined directly into Marshall's pupils.

"How you doing, white shirt?" said a familiar voice.

Marshall blinked several times as the soft features of Marlene's face came into focus. She was accompanied by three people: two women who shared almost identical alabaster skin, green eyes, and thin smiles, whom Marshall immediately assumed were sisters; and a tall, gaunt man with an oversized nose and a crooked mouth that appeared to be the aftermath of an unfortunate altercation.

"Marlene?" Marshall asked, rhetorically.

"The one and only," Marlene replied.

"What are you doing here?"

"We're the welcoming committee. Dad wanted to make sure you had a familiar face when you got here. This is Lewis and these are the twins, Anna and Natasha."

"Mom had a thing for Russian writers. I'm Anna," said the woman on the left, who was wearing black, form fitting khaki pants and an olive green t-shirt. Marshall had no idea what she was referring to regarding Russian writers, but deemed it best not to ask.

"We're not actually twins. I'm older by almost a year, said the woman on the right, whom Marshall presumed to be Natasha.

He glanced at Lewis, awaiting some sort of introduction, which did not come. After a moment Marshall said, "I'm Marshall."

"Yeah, we know," said Anna. "Eric told us all about you."

"Lost puppy," Marlene chimed in.

"Alright, enough with the pleasantries. Time to move," Natasha cut in.

Only then did Marshall begin to take in his surroundings. He was in a basement room about eight feet long by twelve feet wide with stone walls that looked to be decaying before Marshall's eyes. Four lamps shaped like upside down bowls hung from the ceiling emitting an eerie yellow light. An imposing large metal door stood at the other end of the room. The air was stale but cool and smelled of dirt.

Natasha walked over to the door and the rest followed behind her. To the side of the door was a keypad and a retinal scanner.

"Aren't those..." Marshall began.

"No, the scanner isn't connected to Skeyelink. We have our own system. Don't worry, they can't see us."

Natasha punched in several numbers, which Marshall could not see, and bent over slightly so the scanner could see her right eye. Marshall heard a loud snap as the lock to the door, which he surmised from the sound was quite extensive, flipped open.

"Don't ever try to get in there without knowing the code," Marlene said quietly to Marshall. "Three wrong tries and the entire building blows up, collapsing this entire room with you in it."

Marshall looked at her dumbfounded as the twins and Lewis filed through the now open door.

"You're kidding."

"Am I?"

"You're not kidding."

"Seriously, three wrong tries and the whole building blows up," Marlene smiled at him again and extended her arm toward the open doorway, inviting Marshall in. Marshall, now unsure if he was standing below a deathtrap, glanced quickly around the room looking for wires or explosives. Seeing nothing but stone and mortar, Marshall stepped through the doorway and onto a landing, after which was a switchback staircase made of concrete with metal railings. He leaned over the railing to look down. The dizzying stairway seemed like an optical illusion, reaching down infinitely into the depths of the earth.

"Where does this go?"

"Down. Long way. Better start walking," Marlene replied as she muscled the heavy metal door shut.

Marshall began following the twins and Lewis down the stairs. He heard Marlene behind him. Although they all seemed to be walking quietly, their steps echoed up and down the staircase.

A myriad of questions began rattling around Marshall's mind. *How many people are in The Resistance? What's at the end of this staircase? How long have you been in The Resistance? Where's Eric?*

What am I going to do in The Resistance? Are you behind all the terrorist activity they're always talking about?

But after the fourth switchback, no one had said a word, and Marshall decided it was best that he not be the one to break the silence. By the time they reached the bottom, Marshall was completely out of breath.

"Going to have to get this one in the gym," Anna said with a grin.

There was another door identical to the one at the top of the stairs. Once again, Natasha punched in a code and scanned her right eye and the door clicked open. The group stepped through into a long hallway, also made of concrete, that ran to the left and the right. Pipes ran up and down the ceiling and the sides of the walls. Two dim yellow lights hung about twenty feet apart on either side. Beyond the lights was utter darkness.

"Catch your breath, we have a bit of a walk," Marlene said.

"Where are we?" Marshall asked.

"Tunnels that connect the old Metrorail lines," Marlene replied.

"I didn't know these still existed."

"Oh, they shut down the trains decades ago and caved in some of the tunnels, but they didn't get them all."

"Why did they shut down the trains?"

"They were expensive to run, and the wealthy didn't use them. Why waste money and resources on people that aren't rich, right? There were lots of projects that were good for the people, good for the planet, that he shut down specifically to save the country money, all while giving his rich friends more. HAP just started touting lines about how the noise of the metro caused cancer or something like that and they shut it all down. Didn't make much sense at the time but then again most of the things he says don't if you take half a second to really think about it."

"How'd you get in here? That staircase couldn't have always been there."

"Wasn't easy. Took a long time. That staircase took over a year to dig out. Didn't help that we had to do it in secret. Wasn't like we could haul away the dirt by the dump truck either. But like I said, we have a lot of skilled people. Installed all these lights using nuclear batteries from old phones."

Marshall confusedly looked at the four lights he could see. The twins and Lewis started walking to the right and as soon as they reached the second light, another light beyond it sputtered to life.

"They turn on when one of these comes within a few feet of them," Anna said, holding up a small black device about the size of a bar of soap. She then placed it back in her pocket.

Marshall and Marlene followed the trio in front of them. Every few seconds, the lights behind them shut off, bathing the path behind them in a heavy blackness. Marshall paused for a second and looked back into the void, realizing that he was walking away from everything he had ever known with every step.

"Stay close," Marlene said. "Get lost down here and chances are you'll never make it out. If you wander into a tunnel that isn't lit, you're done for."

Marshall quickened his pace.

"How long have you been part of this?"

"I was born into it."

"And your parents? Eric and Coretta?"

"My parents are some of the original group, at least in DC. I mean, The Resistance grew everywhere, all at once. It's human nature to fight against tyranny. Oppression requires obedience. The second you realize that, it's hard to remain willfully subservient. From day one, people resisted. It used to be that people would march in the streets by the millions against him and his fascist regime. There was a time when people thought it would only last a few years, and that his whole party would be voted out the next election and sanity would be restored. But there were no more free elections after he came to power. He quickly built up HALE, recruited all the right people that were prone to racism and violence, and before anyone could blink, there were troops patrolling major cities across the country, especially the cities led by people who opposed him."

"Wait, there weren't always troops in the cities?"

"Of course not. We were a free country once. But he declared emergency after emergency. He declared an economic emergency and claimed powers to place tariffs on other countries. He declared that the nation was being invaded by immigrants and claimed the power to arrest anyone he wanted and disappear them without trial. He claimed crime emergencies in cities where there was no emergency and put troops in those cities to control the people there. None of these emergencies were real, but he did it anyway to gain more and more power. Before anyone knew it, there were masked men kidnapping people off the streets and armed soldiers patrolling our major cities."

The trio in front suddenly took a left down another tunnel. Marshall did not see any signage on the wall to indicate where they were going and wondered how they knew this was the correct tunnel to go down.

"Why didn't anyone stop him?"

"People tried. The problem is, the country had a system of government based on checks and balances that assumed those in charge, those elected into power, would respect the system, and abide by the rules that the founders of the country set forth. But when you have someone become president who doesn't care about the rules, or doesn't even know the rules, and decides to start doing things that are fundamentally against everything the country stood for, it becomes hard to stop him."

"Checks and balances?"

"There used to be three branches of government. The president headed the executive, congress wrote the laws, and the courts could determine what laws were constitutional. The problem when HAP came to power was congress was completely in his control. The courts did fight back a little, but the courts didn't have their own police force, so they relied on the president to execute their orders. And the president had already stacked the highest court with loyalists. The president had control of the military and the federal law enforcement and at the end of the day, if he didn't like what the courts ordered, he simply decided to ignore them. Clearly, he wouldn't follow through on orders that stymied his own power."

"What happened during the elections?"

"Well, there used to be a law that the president could only be president twice, for 8 years total. But close to the end of his second term, he decided to invade Canada. He claimed he had information that Canada was going to attack the country and he had to stop it before they did. Of course, like most of the things he claimed, he never showed any evidence of this. With a war right at our border, he claimed another emergency and unilaterally revoked the twenty-second amendment, claiming the country would fail if a new commander in chief were installed during the middle of the war. The next time there were elections, his party rigged them so there was no way for him to lose. And that was that."

"You were there for all this? You saw all of this?"

"No, I was born afterwards, like you. But my dad was. He was just a kid at the time. My grandparents explained it all to him, made sure he understood from an early age what exactly was happening."

They made another turn and Marshall was sure he would never be able to find his way out without their guidance at this point.

"You used the word fascist. I saw that word in a book your dad gave me but I'm not sure what it means."

"It's an extreme nationalist ideology where all power is centralized at the top, usually with a dictator. It depends on a strong military force to suppress dissenting voices through violence. Although, they can also use other tools like economic pressure to ensure no one steps out of line. Fascists will pit groups against each other to gain power. Generally, it's built on the lie that certain races and religions are superior to others. It then centralizes power by pitting the majority against minorities. Hitler did it by demonizing the Jews and anyone that wasn't part of the Aryan race. The HAP did it by demonizing immigrants, Muslims, and transgender people. But it's the same old playbook."

"Alright textbook, we're almost there," Natasha interrupted.

"Textbook?" Marshall asked.

"Schools used to have these things called textbooks," Anna explained, "They were used to teach kids about history, math, science, all kinds of things. Marlene here is our very own walking, talking textbook. At least she sounds like one when she starts explaining things."

"I get it from my dad. Plus, this isn't my first time and you're not my first pupil," Marlene responded, giving Marshall a wink and a smile. He felt a flutter in his stomach he could not explain.

The group of five turned another corner, the lights continuing to quietly flash on above them as they walked forward. Suddenly they came upon another metal door. Natasha looked up above the door and waived. Marshall looked in the same direction but saw nothing.

"Miniaturized cameras. We have them everywhere down here. No one comes in or out without us knowing about it," Marlene explained.

"They've been watching us this whole time?"

"Yup. State of the art. You won't be able to spot the cameras if you tried, but we can see you, even in the dark."

"Where'd you get all this stuff? I thought only the government was allowed to own surveillance equipment."

"Bingo."

"You stole it all from the government?"

"You catch on quick."

"How?"

"We have people everywhere. Like I said before, tyranny will automatically breed resistance, even from within."

There was a loud click, the door slid open and the five of them stepped inside. Marshall could not believe his eyes. Behind was a massive room buzzing with activity. Above was an arched ceiling, honeycombed with rectangular insets that appeared to be made of concrete. The floor was made of brick on two sides and in the middle was metal grating that appeared to cover a trench, which split the area in two, down the middle. This ended on either side of the cavernous room at brick walls that were clearly put in place more recently. Marshall assumed these were the old tunnels that the trains ran through, but he had never seen them before so he could not be sure.

To his left, there were at least a dozen desks with extra large monitors placed on each one. A grid of images rotated through each monitor, clearly video surveillance of some kind. Several people sat at the bank of monitors, watching the video feeds. To his right there was a phalanx of tables filled with people. At first glance, they were a ragtag mixture of men, women and children. Most were animatedly talking with others, while some looked quiet and forlorn. Something looked odd about these people and at first, Marshall was not sure what it was. Then he quickly realized that they were mostly engaging with each other, rather than staring at their own phones, which Marshall assumed had all been confiscated before entering The Nest.

Most had plates of food in front of them and were eating. Seeing them made Marshall aware of the smells of roasting meats and vegetables that were mixing with the damp, concrete cave smell of the tunnels. There was no obvious kitchen, but he assumed there must be a large one somewhere to feed this many people.

On the other side of the cavern were rows upon rows of shelving. To the left the shelving was filled with supplies. To the right there were grow lights above each shelf and the whole area was bathed in green leaves.

"Welcome to The Nest," Marlene said.

The area was obviously soundproofed, as the tunnel he had just come in from was dead silent, yet there was plenty of noise in here. Marlene closed the door behind them with a thud.

"How is this possible? Where do all these people come from? What are they all doing here?" Marshall's questions spilled out like water rushing from an overfilled glass.

"Years and years of hard work. These people? We come from everywhere. We are everyone. Orphans, mothers, young, old, the strong and the sick, and anyone that doesn't fit into HAP's plan for America. Anyone who sees the reality of injustice and has the courage to not accept it as status quo. Refugees and fighters, and anyone in need. Everyone is vetted, of course, one way or another. People don't just find their way in here."

"Aren't you worried they'll find you? How do you keep such a huge place hidden?"

"Oh, we're worried every day. But we've taken precautions. And all the tunnels leading here for miles are lined with our own cameras. Anyone comes anywhere near this place and we'll know about it."

"And then what? What if they show up and you see them coming?"

"Remember what I said about that house blowing up if you enter the wrong code?"

Marshall nodded.

"Yeah, I wasn't kidding."

"Seriously?"

"We have to protect ourselves. Come on, I'll show you where you'll be staying."

"I'm staying here?"

"You can't go home. Where else you going to go?"

"I guess...I guess I don't have anywhere else."

"No one does. Come on."

Marlene led Marshall across the great hall. Several people nodded to her as they walked by. It was not until they started crossing the metal grating that covered the old train tracks that Marshall noticed Lewis and The Twins were no longer with them.

"Where'd Lewis and The Twins go?"

"They have other duties to attend to."

"I see..."

"You're joining us at a pretty hectic time, Marshall."

"What do you mean?"

"Well, we've been planning something pretty big for a long time now, and we're just a few weeks away."

"The attack on Facts? On Skeyelink?"

Marlene paused her steps and looked him in the eye. Her breath held for a second. Then her shoulders relaxed.

"Dad must really see something in you."

"Huh?"

"Dad's not a big mouth. Not by a long shot. The fact that he told you that...before you even got here, well that's surprising. But if dad trusts you with that, then there must be something here."

"I don't understand."

"Neither do I. Come on, white shirt, I'll show you the barracks and then show you where to get some grub. I'm starving."

12

The barracks was a simple rectangular room with about six dozen bunk beads lined up in four rows with minimal space between each. There was one large bathroom with several stalls and showers, and a massive room full of clothes organized by size. Marshall was happy to take a shower and afterwards found an old pair of jeans, and a gray short sleeve shirt with the outline of a bird holding an arrow in its beak screen printed on the front that fit him relatively well. The jeans were slightly uncomfortable at first, since he was used to wearing khakis, but he got used to them within a few minutes.

The kitchens turned out to be behind another room at the end of the old station. They were serving a hearty chicken noodle soup and some toasted bread. He sat at one of the tables as Marlene went and got them both a bowl. She returned after a few minutes with two mismatched bowls, steam wisping above both, balanced on a single tray. She sat opposite him, placed one bowl in front of him, the other in front of herself, and began to eat.

Marshall had no idea he was as hungry as he was until he brought the first spoonful of soup to his mouth. There seemed to be real pieces of chicken in the soup, not the processed slabs of meat he was used to in his standard ration meals. The flavor was heavenly. Unlike the processed chicken he normally ate, this chicken did not dissolve into mealy bits the second he began chewing on it, and Marshall savored each bite like it might be his last.

After several minutes, Marshall asked, "where does The Resistance get its food? This is the best chicken I've ever had."

"Good right? Not like that shit you get from the HAP's ration packs. No, this is real food from real farms."

"You guys have real farms? Where?"

"No, *we* don't. We prefer to let the HAP do our work for us. You're eating bonafide presidential chicken right there. We figure, why should he get to keep all the best food for himself. He's not going to eat all of it anyway."

"Like the cameras?"

"Yup, liberated from presidential farms that are mostly unknown to the public. We're the Robin Hood of poultry," she said with a smile.

"Who's Robin Hood?"

"Old story. A thief. A good thief. Robbed from the rich and gave to the poor. A story the HAP doesn't want you to know about. Might give you funny ideas about equality and economic justice. So obviously it's gone now."

"I see." Marshall took several more bites as he quietly tried to wrap his thoughts around an uneasy feeling.

"How is it possible that you're able to steal so much from the government and get away with it? You steal so much as a candy bar and HALE will erase you in an instant."

"That's the world you've built in your head, Marshall. Or, more accurately, that's the world they've built in your head. They're not as powerful as you think. Their power stems from your willingness to believe in it. Plus, they're arrogant. They've been telling everyone the same lies for so long they probably actually believe them. They believe they're all powerful, unstoppable. That nothing can bring them down. Any time there's a successful operation, a Resistance operation, they sweep it under the rug so the population doesn't see their incompetence. And when one fails, they make a huge deal of it to strike fear in the people that the boogeyman is lurking behind every corner, but also to show that only the HAP can protect us all."

"The boogeyman?"

"We're the boogeyman, Marshall."

"And every time there's some sort of raid or attack, it's always you?"

"No. Actually, when you hear about it, more often it's not us. Not formally anyway. But it is The Resistance in a way, in that anyone who does anything to fight back against the HAP is part of The Resistance, whether they know it or not."

"But sometimes it's you."

"Sometimes, yes. And sometimes we don't know. There are pockets of Resistance all over the country. Some are big operations, some are just a few people in a bunker. And there's no centralized command. No one person knows everything or everyone. And it's important we keep it that way."

"Why? Wouldn't it make more sense if there was more coordination?"

"Too much coordination can be analyzed. Too much coordination leads to predictability. And we're all liable to be picked up at any time. So too much centralization leads to a vulnerability that we really can't afford. One cell goes down, it can't take others with it. We're the opposite of them, of the HAP. Of consolidation of all power. For the HAP, all power flows through the top. And that's their greatest weakness."

"And you've been doing this your whole life?"

"Pretty much. How about you? Dad told me you don't talk much about yourself."

"Not much to tell really."

"Where you from?"

"Here, I guess."

"You guess?"

Marshall could feel his body tense up like a knot in a rainstorm. It was the same reaction he always felt when his past became the topic of conversation, or even when his mind wandered into that realm.

"Yeah. I grew up in a PCRF."

"I see. So your parents were erased?"

"My parents?"

"Yeah, you know, the people that donated some DNA to the cause of bringing you into this world."

"I didn't have any parents."

"Ah, I see. So they were erased."

"I...don't know. I...I can't remember."

"I'm sorry to hear that, Marshall," Marlene said with genuine empathy.

"I, I get flashes sometimes. When I'm dreaming, mostly. Flashes of some people that I think might be my parents. But by the time I wake up, they're gone.

"I hope some day they come back to you."

"I don't know. Easier this way isn't it?"

"That's what they want you to think. Easier for who? For you? Or for them?"

"I...I guess for them?"

"You asking me?"

"I don't know."

"How old are you, Marshall?"

"Thirty-six."

"About time you figured it out, don't you think?"

At this, Marshall bristled. The tension in his chest unraveled and suddenly he found himself standing up. In that moment, he felt like a battered animal, cornered and desperate, frightened and alone.

"You know, this isn't easy for me. I was fine, going about my own life until your dad showed up, you know. Now I'm here, scared for my life, hiding out underground. What am I even doing here?"

Marlene smiled at him. "So there is some blood under that creamy skin of yours. Now my dad didn't just show up. You walked through his door, remember?"

"Yeah...but...I didn't ask for this."

"You want to go back?"

"I can't go back."

"True. But if you could, would you?"

"I...I guess not."

"Right. So here we are."

Marshall paused for a second. He then realized several people at the tables around him were looking at him. Marshall sat down meekly.

"I guess you're right."

"You sure do guess a lot, Marshall. Listen, ignorance is bliss for the ignorant. But not all of us have that luxury. You lived your life, ignorant of all the pain, all the suffering that people like me endure. So yeah, I'm sure things were fine for you. You had food, you had a job, you had an apartment. Not great, from what I understand, but it was a life. But now you've seen the truth, you've seen the other side, there's no more ignorance to hide behind. Welcome to the real world."

Marshall sat, dumbfounded for several seconds, knowing she was right but not fully wanting to admit it to himself. Finally, Marlene broke the silence.

"Tell me about the PCRF."

"It was wonderful," Marshall replied automatically.

"Bullshit."

"What do you want me to say?"

"Tell me about the PCRF."

"I...I don't want to talk about it."

"Why not? Too wonderful?"

"It was shit, alright? Happy?"

"No, Marshall. I'm not happy. But it's important to talk about it truthfully. Tell me about it."

Marshall took a moment to collect his thoughts. Then he began: "Every day was a nightmare. Every night we'd all go to bed scared. Have you ever felt utterly alone in a room filled with hundreds of people? That was my life, every single day, alright? Is that what you want to hear?"

"No, Marshall, it's not about what I want to hear. It's about what you want to face. You're not the first person to come through here that had their family erased. You're not the first person to survive a PCRF. You hide from yourself behind a curtain of self-imposed ignorance and hope to make it through to the next day. Guess what? Some day, the next day is going to catch up to you. You'll either face your past, and face the present or you'll die a hollowed out shell that they've worked so hard to turn you into."

Again, Marshall sat quietly, not knowing what to say or how to even think. Marlene also sat quietly, knowing Marshall needed the space to think through what she said.

Finally, after several minutes, Marshall spoke up.

"There were hundreds of us in that PCRF. I was put there really early. I can't remember how old I was. Too young to know how old I was, maybe. We stayed in these big rooms with about twenty beds in each room. Every day was regimented, every second was scheduled. You had a time to wake up, a time to eat breakfast, a time to shower, classes, exercise, our whole lives laid out before us. Even though I was surrounded by other kids, there was no play. We had sports, where we had to compete with each other, but that's it. There were no friendships. The ones that tried to form friendships disappeared quickly. Placed in other PCRFs, perhaps, or who knows.

"I remember one kid. I don't even remember his name. I remember when he came in. We were maybe eleven or twelve? I don't remember. Anyway, he was put in the bed next to mine. At first, he was quiet. Scared. Like everyone was when they first came in. Well, I guess like everyone was all the time. I remember him crying that first night. Quietly, to himself. I doubt anyone else heard, or if they did, no one said anything. I didn't say anything either, of course. Didn't even look him in the eyes in the morning. I mean, I mostly kept to myself anyway, so that wasn't any different than normal.

"At breakfast he must have recognized me from being in the bed next to his, because he deliberately sat next to me. He asked me my name. I told him and he gave me his. But then he started asking questions about the place. Questions about how the place was run, who the adults were, what the other kids were like. There was no rule against talking to the other kids during mealtimes, but you never knew which topics were off limits, and if you crossed a line they would punish you. No one ever talked about the punishments, but the kids that were taken out, they always came back quiet. You never saw any bruises or cuts, or anything like that, but they came back...different. More scared. More...withdrawn inside themselves. And early on I knew I didn't want to find out what had been done to them. So, I answered some of his questions but for the most part just tried to keep my mouth shut, because we all knew they were listening all the time.

"And then he brought up his father. He had been erased just a few days before. He began telling me the story. I don't know why. It's not like I asked him or anything, but he seemed the type that just needed to talk. He didn't get too far into it before one of the adults came in and pulled him out. And that was it. We all sat with our heads down staring at our food as he kicked and screamed trying to stay at the table while the soldiers dragged him out of the cafeteria.

"The next time I saw him was two days later. He climbed into his bed about an hour after lights out. He didn't cry that night. He didn't say anything the next morning. He just looked...dazed. He would still sit next to me during meals. But he didn't talk. Just stared off into space. He didn't eat much either. I noticed that. Not that he was missing much. The food was terrible. About a week later he disappeared. Never saw him again.

"That was what it was like in the PCRF."

Marlene nodded knowingly. "Sorry you had to go through that, Marshall."

Marshall looked down at his bowl of soup, which was quickly losing its heat. He picked up the spoon and finished off the rest. Marlene followed suit and they ate in silence. Marshall, for one, was used to that.

13

The next week went by quickly. There were several clocks around The Nest, but without the cadence of sunrises and sunsets, time seemed to slip by like grains of sand through his fingers. Marshall was given several choices of where he could help out and he chose the kitchen. Each day, he helped prepare all three meals, and each evening he had dinner with Marlene so she could bring him up to speed on hundreds of years of human history, political philosophy, and science that he had never been exposed to.

Aside from these meals, which he looked forward to most of all, Marshall loved his job. The kitchen atmosphere was exhilarating. In his entire life, Marshall does not remember cooking a single meal. Everything he ate, starting from when he was in the PCRF, was a standard food ration. Not once had he chopped vegetables, browned real meat, or even cracked an egg.

Charlotte, the tall, red headed head chef, took Marshall under her wing and taught him the basics, like how to curl his fingers back when using a knife, how to dice onions properly, and how to check to see if a pan is hot enough to start cooking. The learning curve was steep. Despite her instructions, Marshall cut himself several times before he got the hang of a chef's knife. But the pain his fingers endured were more than made up for by the novel feelings he had when in the kitchen.

The bustling atmosphere of the kitchen was the exact opposite of the solitary cubicle he had spent the majority of his adult life in. It was the first time in his life he felt like he was on a team of people, all with one singular purpose. It was hot and chaotic, with people moving around him at all times, talking over each other, laughing, singing, and swearing. Marshall loved it all.

There was a rhythm to the kitchen that Marshall could sense but at first could not pick up. He was given menial tasks, which he performed gratefully and quietly, all while soaking in the vibe. But after a few days, something clicked in his mind. Jokes that made no sense to him at first, became second nature and predictable. He found himself quietly singing along to songs that the chefs repeated, without realizing he had learned the words.

Despite this, there was a part of Marshall that still felt isolated. It was not for lack of trying, both from his end and from the rest of the kitchen staff, to fully bring him into the fold. Gregory, an older man with long white hair and small, half-moon spectacles, spoke with him often, but Marshall fell into his familiar role of listener and only chimed in when asked direct questions. Charlotte checked in on him often, teaching by showing and giving him tips on the tasks he was given. Marcus, a younger man in his midtwenties with sparkling eyes and a devious smile, told jokes to Marshall that the rest of the staff had clearly heard before as they often groaned in response when he started them. Marshall only got half the jokes but the telling of the jokes seemed more the point than drawing a laugh for Marcus. Regardless of these overtures, it always felt like there was some sort of barrier for Marshall. As if he had jumped into a pond, was swimming happily, but for whatever reason was unable to fully submerge his head.

The recipes were basic. Mostly, they made soups and stews, which were easy to make in large batches for many people. By the end of the first week, Marshall was surprised at how quickly he had acclimated to his new life. He did not think much about his old job, the people that he worked with, his old apartment, or anything else beyond what his daily tasks were. He figured this lack of thought toward the life he so abruptly walked away from was an indicator that he did not miss much about it.

On the seventh day in The Nest, Marshall saw Eric for the first time since he had left the antique store a week prior. It was around 4:00 in the afternoon and Marshall was at his station, chopping carrots for a turkey casserole they were making when Eric walked into the kitchen. He was immediately greeted by Charlotte.

"Eric, long time! Where you been all my life?" Charlotte joked.

"Been standing right here!"

Charlotte walked over and the two embraced in a long hug. Marshall stayed where he was, watching the interaction, but he could feel a smile solidify on his own face. It was clear that they were old friends.

"How's the shop?" Charlotte asked.

"Old. Old like me," Eric replied

"Well, you look pretty good for a hundred and fifty," Charlotte laughed.

"If Coretta hears about you flirting with me, you'll end up in that casserole you're making over there!"

"Just like old times, having your wife fight your battles for you."

"Only when I want to win," Eric laughed again.

"It's good to see you."

"You too. How's our new recruit?" Eric scanned the kitchen for a second until his eyes fell on Marshall.

Marshall smiled. It felt good to be recognized.

"Heard he was cooking up a storm in here."

"He's a regular Julia Childs." Marshall had no idea who that was but took it as a compliment.

"Bet he is," Eric said as he turned toward Marshall.

Marshall put down his knife as Eric walked over and they shook hands.

"How are you doing, here in The Nest?" Eric asked.

"Fine. A little different from my apartment."

"Very." Eric looked over to Charlotte, "Charlotte, can I borrow this chef?"

"Just make sure you get him back in one piece. Those onions aren't going to chop themselves."

"You got it."

Eric looked back at Marshall.

"Come with me."

"Where we going?"

"You'll see," Eric responded and led Marshall out of the kitchen, through the main hall, and out the large main door he first came in a week ago. The dark tunnel immediately lit up the second they stepped through.

As soon as they were through the door, Eric clapped Marshall on the back and smiled.

"So really, how are you?" He asked as he started walking. Marshall walked by his side.

"Good, I think. Really enjoying this cooking thing. Still getting used to it down here. How are things topside?" Marshall responded, instinctively changing the subject away from himself.

"Same old, same old. Grinding away slowly."

"What does that mean?"

"We all have jobs. Mine, among other things, is recruitment. So I'm out recruiting."

"People like me?"

"Well, yes and no. It's a slow process and we can't be too careful."

Marshall then asked a question that had been bugging him ever since Eric first took him downstairs below the antique store. "How did you know I was going to walk into your store?"

"What do you mean?"

"I mean, how did you recruit me?"

"Oh, Marshall, I didn't. You did. I had no idea who you were when you walked into my store. Most of the time we do our research, find likely candidates, and vet them over months and months before we reveal ourselves. But you? You just walked in on your own. I had a sense about you from the beginning, and when you came back the next week with that watch, it was clear you had some moral backbone. I just had to see how much."

"You mean all of this happened by accident?"

"Most of life is an accident Marshall. Right place, right time. Wrong place, wrong time. You'd be surprised how much of your life is dictated by luck, both good and bad. Had you been ten feet farther down the street when you spotted that guy you were hiding from, you'd have ducked into a different spot, or just had to talk to him, and you'd be at your cubicle right now erasing people. Those ten feet led you here."

"And what accident led you here?"

"Birth. The accident of who my parents were. That's the real luck of the draw. You have no choice who your parents are going to be, which is important to remember. Some people are born into wealth and luxury, some are born into hunger and poverty. And every one of us could easily have been born into a very different situation. The lucky could have just as easily been unlucky. Which is why it is important to have empathy for those with less than yourself. Their life could have easily been yours."

"What is empathy?"

"It means drawing from your own experience and feelings to understand someone else's feelings and thoughts about something. It's a word that they phased out, deleted from dictionaries, and took out of the public vocabulary, because they claimed it was a made-up new age word that does a lot of damage. But the reality is they hate the word because it describes something that is antithetical to their strategy of dividing the masses. It's hard to demonize and dehumanize marginalized groups of people if people can feel empathy for them. So, they got rid of the word."

Marshall thought for a moment, and then went back to a question that weighed on him from a moment ago: "Do you mean everyone who is rich and powerful was born rich and powerful? What about the American dream? Some people are able to move up. That happens all the time!"

"Does it? Does it happen all the time? It happens sometimes. The dream is that it could happen to anyone. But the reality is that it can happen to almost no one. And to join the class of the ultrawealthy? Well that's basically impossible. Even those who move up have been born into circumstances that helped them do so. It was more possible when I was young. But it has gotten harder and harder every year as the rich have consolidated more and more of the wealth. There's only a certain amount of wealth in this world at any given time. If most of it is in the hands of a very few, then there's not enough for everyone else, is there? Certainly not enough for people to move up in the world.

The fascinating thing is those born into wealth and power often grow to believe they deserve it, that they earned it. And if they believe that, then they must believe the poor, the lower classes deserve their station in life too. Of course, most people cannot escape the situation they're born into, both lucky and unlucky, despite what they tell you about the American dream. But those born into wealth, born into power, will justify the injustice and inequity of our system because they are on top, because they won the birth lottery. And so they spout the fiction of the American dream to make people below them believe they too, can become rich and powerful, when in reality the vast majority cannot. This fiction helps them justify their own station as one that is earned, and not one that is lucky and built on the backs of the hardworking people beneath them."

The two walked on, making turns every now and then. Marshall followed Eric's lead, unaware of the direction they were going or for how long they had walked. With each step he processed the words Eric preached, which were continuing to tear down his understanding of the world, brick by brick.

Finally Marshall asked, "Where are we going?"

"Good timing. We're going right here."

They turned one more corner and stepped into a pitch black corridor. The lights from the tunnel behind them showed a dead end about 20 feet in front and a pile of rotting wood stacked up against the wall. Then the lights behind them shut off and they were bathed in darkness. Marshall's stomach jumped and panic flooded his mind.

"Eric? Eric?" Marshall said quickly in succession and reached out to where Eric had been standing. Relief came suddenly as he felt Eric's shoulder.

"Hold on, Marshall. Sorry about that. Should've warned you."

A moment later the corridor lit up from a pocket lantern Eric held in his hand. What Marshall saw in the seconds before the lights behind him shut off was confirmed. They stood in a dank, stone corridor that ended about twenty feet in front, at a stone wall. Several pieces of rotting wood leaned up against the wall in front of them.

"What are we doing here?" Marshall asked.

"A promise is a promise," Eric replied, walking towards the wooden beams. He then placed the pocket lantern on the ground and said, "Come, help an old man move these."

"Move them where?"

"Just lean them off to the side here."

Eric moved some of the smaller pieces of wood, leaning them against the side wall, and Marshall followed suit, choosing the larger, heavier pieces. After a few moments, the wall was cleared of wood. Marshall looked at the wall, which was damp and looked old, as if it had been undisturbed for generations.

"I still don't see what..."

Eric pulled one of the stones and it swung open to the left as if on a hinge. Behind it was a palm reader. Eric looked at Marshall and smiled and winked. He placed his hand on the palm reader and said "Eric Blair."

There was a soft click, and a rattling sound, and then the stone wall split. Several of the stones in the middle swung outwards and a doorway formed.

"Not everything is as it seems," Eric said to Marshall with a wink. He picked up the pocket lantern and walked through the doorway. Marshall followed close behind as they emerged into a cavernous room. He could see shelving in front of him that seemed to go on forever but the pocket lantern was not bright enough to extend beyond a few rows. The air inside felt dry and cool and smelled of cement and another odor that tickled Marshall's memory, but which he could not place. Eric closed the door behind them and Marshall saw that the rocks were attached to a large metal door with an intricate locking mechanism behind it.

"What is this place?" Marshall asked.

"Just a moment," Eric replied, and took a few steps to the left until he reached a large switch on the wall. He pulled it down and the room was ablaze with light. Rows upon rows of books revealed themselves from the darkness.

"Welcome to The Library, or as I like to call it, The Cemetery of Forgotten Books."

Marshall was flabbergasted. Suddenly he recognized the aroma that had wafted into his nose. It was the same smell he smelled when he opened "It Can't Happen Here." The smell was heavenly.

"Told you I'd bring you. This is our most prized possession. Keeping this place safe is one of our most important missions. Not everyone in the resistance knows about this place and those who do must swear that they will never utter a single word about it to anyone, that they will protect it with their lives if necessary."

"Ha...ha...have you read all these?"

Eric laughed. "It would take me a hundred lifetimes to read all these. But if I had that time, I would certainly try. Now Marshall, promise me you'll protect this place. That you won't tell a soul, even to other people in The Resistance, unless you're one hundred percent certain they know about it, and even then, only when you're one hundred percent certain you're absolutely alone."

"I don't understand. I mean, this is amazing. It's...it's the most amazing thing I think I've ever seen. But why is it that important?"

"Remember what I told you, about how they have built a world in your head that doesn't exist?"

Marshall nodded.

"Ignorance is their greatest ally. Lies are their best friend. And not having an alternative to the stories they tell is what they depend on. If everyone is only fed their lies, then their lies become truth and the real world melts away. It's why, when all this began, they started trying to ban certain books from schools and libraries. It all led to the Great Digitization. At the end of the day, no matter what we do, the only way we can tear down their tyranny is by showing people the truth."

Eric swept his right hand out towards the shelves of books.

"This is the truth. Within these books is the history they've tried to forget. Within these books is the science they've tried to erase. Knowledge is the mortal enemy to authoritarianism and the key to freedom. We must guard it and keep it safe. Promise me."

Marshall nodded again, feeling a gravity of the situation that he did not fully understand. "I promise," he said.

"Good, then you may explore."

"Explore?"

"Sure, go on, take a stroll. Walk around. Browse. Peruse. Grab a book or two. Take your time."

"Where will you be?"

"Right here, in my chair."

Eric took a few more steps over and Marshall saw several armchairs that he had not noticed before. Behind each armchair a lamp curved overhead, like a swan craning its neck over the chair. Next to them was a small bookshelf. Eric leaned over, grabbed a book, and sat down in the nearest armchair. He reached behind him, flicked on the light and promptly started reading.

Marshall slowly began walking towards the shelves. As he did he looked around. Upon walking into The Library, his eyes only drank in the endless shelves of books. But now he also saw the grandeur of the place. There were stone columns every fifteen feet. Arches formed between each column, crisscrossing all across the ceiling, creating squares the encased slightly sloping domes of rock. It was beautiful.

Upon reaching the books, Marshall noticed immediately that the shelves themselves matched the wooden ones in Blair's Antiques. At the start of each row, hung on the end of the shelf, was a placard. The first one read Fiction, Aa-Ad. It was unclear what this meant. He continued walking down until he reached Fiction Ha-Hi when he decided to turn into the row for no apparent reason. Surrounded by books, Marshall felt a mixture of awe, giddiness, and pride. Awe from the sheer number of books; giddiness at the amount of forbidden knowledge at his fingertips; and pride because Eric had chosen him, trusted him with this knowledge. He also realized in that moment what he did not feel: fear.

Marshall walked down the aisle, his hands slowly caressing the books on either side of him. He felt his fingertips traverse the crevasses between each tome, the notches created when a smaller book was lodged between two larger ones, the smooth glossy paper of some books and the hard, scratchy binding of others. He noticed that some books all had similar fonts and styles and realized that they were by the same author. Were they a series? A collection of stories that were interconnected? He had read very few books in his life, and only the classics on tablets that were forced upon him in the PCRF. He knew only a handful of authors, like Schmitt, Raspail and Pierce. The notion that there were this many people who wrote novels, and that some of them wrote several, even dozens, was incredible.

One particular book caught his eye and he paused. He was not sure why the title drew him in, but it did. Marshall laid his pointer finger on top of the book, pulled it out, and looked at the cover.

"For Whom the Bell Tolls," he said aloud to himself. He turned it over and quietly read the back. After reading the blurb, he turned it over and looked at the front cover again. "Ernest Hemingway," he said. Then he realized what the placards at the end of each row must mean. Quickly he went back to the beginning of the aisle and walked further down until he got to Ky- Li. He walked down until he got to authors beginning with Le. A few more moments and he found a series of Lewis's.

"C.S., Michael," he whispered to himself. "Ah, Sinclair." And there it was. He pulled out the copy of It Can't Happen Here, and then realized he was still holding For Whom the Bell Tolls. Marshall began walking back towards the front with the two books, feeling as if he had won a prize or found a treasure. He found Eric still sitting in the chair quietly reading his book. As he walked over, Eric looked up and glanced at the books in Eric's hand.

"What did you find?" Eric asked.

Marshall showed him the two books.

"Ah, I was wondering if you'd find your way back to that. And Hemingway! Excellent choice. One of my favorite authors."

"Can I take these with me?"

"Sorry, you can't. They stay here. Not everyone in The Nest knows about the Cemetery of Forgotten Books, and if you take a book out in the middle of lunch there's going to be a lot of questions. But you can leave them on this bookshelf and read them here. These chairs are pretty cozy."

"I can come back here?"

"Of course, although you'll need someone to take you. You can ask Marlene or Charlotte. But no one else."

"Okay," Marshall said reluctantly. "Can we stay a bit longer?"

"We should probably head back or Charlotte will kill me. Those onions won't chop themselves, right?"

Marshall, disappointed, took a few steps over and placed his books on the small shelf by the wall. Eric turned off the light behind him and then did the same. The two then walked over to the door they entered from. This side of the door was less complicated. A turn of a lever and the locking mechanism disengaged. Eric pushed the door open, took out his pocket lantern, and the two stepped through. After closing the door, the wall regained its uniform appearance. Marshall helped

Eric place the wooden planks back up against the wall, completing the abandoned look of the supposedly dead end tunnel. They then walked back towards the main tunnel where the lights flickered on. Marshall walked alongside Eric as they made their way back to The Nest.

"Why do you call it the Cemetery of Forgotten Books?" Marshall suddenly asked.

"It comes from one of my favorite series, written by an author named Carlos Ruiz Zafron. Of course, it was banned a long time ago and completely disappeared after the great digitization."

"Why was it banned?"

"Same reason that For Whom The Bell Tolls was banned," Eric said. "Both talk about the Spanish Civil War."

"I don't understand. What was the Spanish Civil War?"

"It was a war in which fascists took over the country of Spain. It was the precursor to World War 2. Hitler actually gave Franco weapons to test out during the fighting before he started World War 2. The fascists won and General Franco, the leader of the fascists, ruled the country for over thirty years after that."

Marshall did not recognize any of these names, but they did not seem to matter. He was more concerned with the books that were banned. "Why was that a reason to ban these books?"

"Because the HAP and his party used the same playbook to take over our country that Hitler did. Demonize a marginalized group of people, blame everyone's problems on that group, and promise that they alone could solve their problems by getting rid of those people. Then once in power, he created made up emergencies to claim powers that don't belong to him, and then never give them back. But they obviously don't want people to know that. So anything about or set in that time period is gone. It's hard to learn from our mistakes when we're never allowed to learn about the mistakes in the first place. But that's enough education for one day. Tell me how you're doing. Really."

Marshall walked on for a few moments, and then sighed.

"I don't know. Really. Part of me misses my apartment, as sad as that sounds. There's always people around down here. I like being alone."

"Do you?"

Marshall thought for another moment. "Well, I guess I'm comfortable being alone."

"It's easy to hide from the world behind the notion of comfort. But sometimes comfort is just the absence of fear. And that's not really comfort."

"I suppose. But now I'm uncomfortable, surrounded by people, and I still feel alone, in a way. There's people all around in The Nest. People talk to me but I'm still alone."

"Life begins where comfort ends, Marshall. That feeling of loneliness comes from within you. You've been taught your entire life that you're alone in this world and so when you're finally surrounded by people who can fill the void, your mind doesn't know what to do with it. But you'll get there."

"Marlene is nice to talk to." The words slipped out of Marshall's mouth before his mind consciously remembered that Marlene was Eric's daughter.

"I'm glad to hear that. I've heard the opposite from some people. But men typically aren't used to strong willed women who speak their minds anymore."

"I think she's the smartest woman I've ever met."

"Marshall, she's probably the smartest *person* you've ever met."

"Including you?"

"By a long shot."

Marshall smiled. "She gets that from you, I bet."

"Nope, her mother."

"Seems like it runs in the family."

"On the women's side really. Let's be fair though, women are naturally more intelligent than men."

Marshall did not know what to say to that. This was the opposite of what he had been taught his entire life. Then again, Marshall's interactions with women have been very limited since he was a child.

"I take it from your silence that you disagree?" Eric asked.

"I don't know what to think these days. Seems like everything I've ever known is wrong."

"Only the lies you've been told to believe. But your gut told you there was something wrong with our country. And that is the most important thing you've ever known. That came from within you. And the fact that you could listen to that reality over everything you've been taught says something."

"What does it say?"

"It says deep down, you're someone who is willing to question what has been force fed to you. It says you have a moral compass that was solidified in you before they could wipe it away. It says that your parents, whoever they were, instilled something in you that they couldn't drive out of you. It says that you're smart, Marshall. You have good instincts. Just make sure you listen to them."

The walk back to The Nest felt faster than the walk to The Library for Marshall. As soon as they got back inside, Eric offered him his hand, which Marshall shook.

"Well, back to the kitchen with you."

"You're leaving already?"

"I have an antiquing empire to run," Eric said with a wink.

"When will you be back?"

"Maybe in a few days. But if you need anything, just talk to Marlene."

"Of course. I will. Thank you, Eric. For everything."

"You're welcome, Marshall. See you soon." With that, Eric turned around and left.

14

The next week went by without incident in The Nest. In those seven days, Marshall helped make scrambled eggs, pancakes, tuna fish sandwiches, spaghetti and meatballs, mashed potatoes, chicken and vegetable stir fry, and several other dishes. Charlotte even began teaching him how to use the stoves.

In the evenings, Marshall's history lessons with Marlene continued. Mostly, they spoke about the history of democracy, and how the world was once ruled by kings and queens, emperors and empresses. She described how over time, common people began demanding rights. She talked about the Magna Carta, the French Revolution, and the American Revolution. She described the United States Constitution and the Bill of Rights, both of which had been altered significantly since the HAP took power. She also discussed more recent history: how the HAP won the presidency and how he eventually was able to absorb so much power into the presidency that no one could oppose him. She described how he used federal powers to coerce spineless businessmen to choose profits over common decency and fundamental morality. How he attacked the media until they bent to his will, leaving Americans little ability to find alternative sources of news, and eventually how he was able to wipe from history anything that disagreed with the narrative that white Christian Americans made this country great.

During that week, Marshall noticed that the lessons had gradually shifted. To start, Marlene did most of the talking, while Marshall asked most of the questions. Over the past few days, Marlene began asking Marshall more questions about his own history and his work as an Eraser. He continued to have trouble discussing his past, and despite his best efforts, was unable to bring up memories of his parents. But he was able to acknowledge he had parents, and that they had been erased, which seemed like a big step for him.

During one of these lessons, Marlene was describing the events that led to a war called "World War 2," which Marshall had only heard about from her father, but knew nothing about.

"There are thousands of reasons and events that lead up to every war, but the long and short of it was this," Marlene described. "Germany was reeling from the Treaty of Versaille, which we talked about a couple days ago. Their economy was struggling, there was hyperinflation, people were hungry and angry. This is when Adolf Hitler stepped in and gave people a place to direct their anger: the Jews. Eventually, he was able to be elected into office by attacking communists, socialists, and minorities. He put his personal troops in the cities, they were called "brownshirts" to terrorize the population and stamp down any opposition. Then, when the Reichstag, that was their congress, burned down, he declared an emergency, claimed the communists were attacking the country, and was eventually able to take full power. As soon as he did, he began passing extremely aggressive policies. He imposed sweeping tariffs on almost all of Germany's trading partners just two weeks after he took power. Of course, these tariffs did not accomplish what he said they would, as any intelligent economist could have told him, but he believed he was smarter than all the experts. He also began building up Germany's military while speaking incessantly about the need for Germany to expand and take over neighboring countries. As a side note, these are all things that the HAP did as soon as he got into office the second time. It's like he was following a blueprint or something...Anyway, eventually, Hitler invaded Poland, and World War 2 began."

"Why do you say 'Hitler invaded Poland?' Didn't the country invade?"

"Sure, you could say Germany invaded Poland. But really, who decides to start a war? In the history of humanity, rarely has a country voted to go to war. Almost all wars started because a few men, or one man, in charge decided it was worth the death of their citizens to attack another group of people."

"Death of their citizens?"

"Well, the number of men who have declared war for their countries and then rode at the head of battle to fight that war are few and far between. More often than not, these men have declared war and then forced the citizens of the country to do the fighting for them."

"I see."

"If the HAP decided it was time to invade Europe, do you think he'd fly over there with a gun and start shooting?"

"Probably not."

"Of course not. He had a chance to fight for his country when he was young and he chickened out like a coward. He pretended he had some minor physical ailment to get out of it. But he would have no problem sending you to die in his name."

"I didn't know any of that."

"No. And you wouldn't. It's all erased from the history books. Just like your folks."

Marshall sat for a moment. This was not the first time Marlene had brought up his parents seemingly out of the blue.

"Right. Just like my parents. How come you keep bringing them up?"

"Because you deserve to know who your parents are. And my guess is, somewhere in that brain of yours, there are memories of them locked away. You've been taught to ignore those memories. Pretend they don't exist. But if we keep trying to rebuild those paths in your brain back to them, eventually maybe you'll remember."

"Let's just get back to..."

At that moment a young woman, whose name Marshall knew to be Josephine, ran up to them, breathing hard, with a panicked look on her face. She was a full head shorter than Marshall but had the body and the mien of a tank. Marshall had seen her around The Nest but had never spoken to her. Even now, when she was clearly agitated, he felt intimidated by her.

"Marlene!"

"What is it Jo? What's wrong?"

"I ran from…I just…your dad!"

Marlene got up immediately. "What? What's wrong with my dad? Spit it out, Jo."

"They…they got your dad."

"WHAT DO YOU MEAN? WHO? WHO GOT HIM? WHERE IS HE?"

"They, Marlene. You know who. He's gone," Jo said at barely a whisper. Marlene slumped back in her chair. Quiet tears began flowing down her face. Marshall could see her hands trembling. He sat there, not knowing what to say or do.

After a moment Marlene wiped the tears from her face, stood back up, and looked directly at Jo. Her expression morphed quickly from despair to determination.

"Where'd they pick him up?"

"The shop."

"And the shop?"

"He was able to blow it before they hauled him out."

"Okay, good. Do we know where they took him? Anyone on the inside make contact yet?"

"No. But probably The Market."

"Then that's that then…" Marlene said. "We need to move up the timeline. We probably have to go sooner than we planned."

"Okay, I'll spread the word." With that, Jo turned around and walked away.

Marlene sat back down and steepled her pointer fingers in front of her face. She closed her eyes and looked deep in thought. Marshall's eyes watched her quietly, but like a hollow jug, his mind was devoid of thought or emotion. He sat still, trying to will himself to comprehend what had just happened. But he could not. It was like he was watching the past few minutes happen to someone else. He could almost see himself in his mind's eye, sitting across from Marlene, as if he was floating above the table.

It was Eric. Eric. The only real friend he had ever had. Gone.

Then the floodgates opened. Marshall lost complete control. His chest heaved as he tried to breath. Tears waterfalled down his face. His vision blurred. His mind became a swamp of despair and anger. His hands clenched into fists. He was overcome by both the urge to attack someone and the desire to sink under the table.

"Marshall," he heard Marlene's voice. "Marshall, it's going to be okay."

Marshall looked through the prism of tears into Marlene's face and suddenly felt shame. He had known Eric for a few months and he was being comforted by his daughter. He forced himself to take a few deep breaths and wiped his face with his hands, clearing the tears from his eyes. Marlene's face was resolute with purpose, and in that moment, was the most beautiful thing Marshall had ever seen.

"We will mourn him later, Marshall. But not now. Now is the time for action."

Marshall stood up as he tried to quell the shuddering aftereffects of his sobbing that were still convulsing his body.

"So...what? Are we going to save him?"

"There's no saving him, Marshall. He would not want us to. Even if we could get him out, the amount of people we would lose to do so would not be worth it."

"Worth it? It's Eric! It's your dad."

"Right. It's my dad. And he wouldn't want us trying something so foolish." She put a heavy hand on his shoulder, which felt grounding. "We're all dead anyway."

Marshall knew she was right, but he did not want to admit it to himself, so he changed subjects.

"What did she mean when she said he blew the shop?"

"Shop's gone, Marshall. The whole thing was rigged to blow in case something like this happened."

"Why? Why destroy the shop?"

"There's a staircase under it coming down to these tunnels. Can't risk them finding it, or at least finding it quickly. Any entry point to these tunnels that we use have to be foolproof. If any of them are compromised, they're blown. Caved in and destroyed."

"Where did..."

"I don't have time to answer all your questions, Marshall. Not right now. I'm sorry. I have to go. There's too much to do. But I'll come back tomorrow. I'll explain it all then. Finish up your dinner and get some rest. The next few days are going to be busy."

With that she turned around and walked away. Only at that moment did Marshall look around. He suddenly became aware of the silence in the massive hall. No one was saying a word and every eye was trained on Marlene as she walked toward the main door. And then he heard a loud wail from the kitchen. It was Charlotte. Word was spreading. Eric had been taken.

15

Marshall barely slept that night. It seemed that everyone knew or knew of Eric and the very air tasted solemn in The Hive. His imagination ran through the worst possible scenarios. Images of Eric chained up in a dark cell, or being beaten and tortured raced through Marshall's mind. He had a feeling that Eric was tougher than his elderly frame looked, but he also worried that there was no way he would be able to withstand the torture that his mind pictured for him.

Marshall's anxiety extended beyond Eric's personal safety. If they were able to draw information out of Eric, everything was in danger. He pictured The Nest being raided by HALE agents. Hundreds of masked, black-suited, gun-toting men bursting through the door and shooting indiscriminately into the old train station. He imagined Charlotte fighting back with one of her kitchen knives only to be shot down. Most worrisome was the idea of Marlene being taken. The idea of her being hurt, killed, or worse made Marshall's skin crawl. He felt protective of her for some reason, even though he knew in reality that if there was a raid, she would be the one protecting him.

In that moment of imagining her suffering at the hands of HALE, Marshall realized he felt something deeper than admiration and respect for her. He was not sure exactly what he was feeling. Perhaps it was friendship. But he was sure he felt friendship for Eric, and this was definitely something different. It was completely novel and unfamiliar. The only things he was sure of were that he missed her when she was not around, felt happier when she was, and he would do anything he could to keep her safe.

And so that night, Marshall laid in bed, ping ponging from sorrow to fear to anger to righteous indignation, as his mind led him on a tour of the worst his imagination could come up with.

After tossing and turning for hours, Marshall got up quietly, so as not to wake anyone in the room. He showered, and got dressed. He was not sure what time it was but decided to head to the kitchen. There were some people in the main station but it was mostly empty. The kitchen seemed empty too at first. Then he saw Charlotte sitting in the corner on a folding chair. One look at her and he knew she also had not slept. Her eyes were bloodshot, her shoulders slouched, and her usual jubilant aura was absent. Marshall looked up at the clock, which read half past four.

"Morning," Charlotte said quietly.

"You're here early."

"Never left."

"You've been here all night?"

Charlotte nodded wearily. She pointed to a couple other folding chairs that were leaning on the wall opposite her. "Grab a chair. Have a seat."

Marshall walked over, grabbed a chair, opened it, and set it down gently next to Charlotte. He could feel the weariness overtaking him as soon as he sat down.

"How long have you known Eric?" Charlotte asked Marshall.

"Just a few months."

"He recruited me seven years ago."

"At the antique shop?"

"No, he came into the restaurant I was working at."

"Cooking?"

Charlotte nodded. "Line cook. Doing what you're basically doing now."

"You should've been the head chef."

"Women don't get to be head chefs, Marshall. Not up there."

Marshall knew that and felt embarrassed for his comment. "Sorry," he murmured.

"Everyone knew I was the best cook in the kitchen. It was a little spot, only a few tables and a bar, but it was always busy. Anyway, there were a few of us that took turns closing the restaurant. You know, putting chairs on tables and making sure the place was locked up. One night, Eric was the last one at the bar, slowly drinking a beer. It was getting late and I wanted to go home, but he started talking and, well, you know how Eric is. Before I knew it, it was almost one in the morning."

Marshall gave a knowing smile. That sounded exactly like Eric.

"You know, my father died when I was young, and..." Charlotte continued.

"Erased?" Marshall interrupted.

"No, not erased. He was away on some trip for business. Was only supposed to be gone for a couple weeks. He did some work with hospitals, medical supplies or something like that. It was at some hospital that he caught the measles. I guess right before he was supposed to come home he started feeling sick. He decided not to come home before he got better. He was scared that he'd give it to us. There were complications and he died before ever making it home."

"I'm sorry."

"Yeah. Well Eric started coming in on the nights I was closing up, just to chat and have a beer. At first I thought it was a little weird but he quickly became like a father to me. Or maybe an older brother. Someone I could trust and would always look out for me. You know?"

"Yeah, I know exactly what you mean."

"After a few months, he introduced me to Marlene. Or had Marlene find me, I guess. The two of them never interact up top. Wasn't long before I found my way to The Nest."

"How many people has Eric recruited for us?"

"Who knows. A lot, I think. He has an eye for who to trust. Who can see past the bullshit. Who knows what's what, you know?"

"I think so..."

"It's a big loss...losing him."

Marshall suddenly felt angry. It seemed like everyone had already given up on Eric. He realized at that moment he was not ready to do that.

"He's not dead yet, right? We can go after him! We can save him!"

"Come on, Marshall. Maybe if we got there when he was being picked up. Out in the open, on the street. Maybe. But once they have him in their facility, well that's a whole 'nother ball game."

Marshall sat for a moment. There had to be a way. "But don't we have people on the inside? Can't we find a way to…"

"Those people on the inside are more valuable staying on the inside. If we blow their cover to get one man out, even if that man is Eric, it's a loss. Eric understands that. The best we can do is slip him something so he can end it himself…"

"But…"

"That's it, Marshall. You're thinking about one man. We're thinking about two hundred million Americans. We have to think about all the people in the camps. We have to think about the mission. We have to think about what's best for the country. And using resources to try to save Eric doesn't help free us from the tyranny of the HAP. Eric knows that better than any of us."

Marshall slumped down in his chair. This was the second person to tell him this. He did not want to accept it but he knew they were right.

"So what's the plan then? Marlene said something about moving up a timeline. Timeline for what?"

"I guess now's as good a time as any…It's time we revealed the man behind the curtain."

"I don't follow."

"Let me ask you a question. Have you ever seen the president with your own eyes?"

"Of course I have, he's on the news every day. He posts on Facts all the time!"

"No, Marshall, with your own eyes."

Marshall thought for a moment. "In person? I don't think so..."

"That's because he's dead. He died decades ago."

"What? No. That can't be right. He gives interviews! He does rallies!"

"No, he doesn't. What they show you is all AI generated. He has holograms that does rallies. He's been dead for decades."

"But the elections!"

"What elections? This country hasn't had a real election in over sixty years."

"No, this isn't possible."

"How old is the president, Marshall?"

"I don't know..."

"Before they altered his bio online, his birth year was 1946."

Marshall thought for a moment. "That would make him...138 years old."

"Precisely."

"But...the Medbeds! He has the only Medbed in the world and it cures all diseases. He said so himself."

"Seems unbelievable doesn't it?"

"I...I guess."

"Because it is."

"Then why has no one said anything? If it's unbelievable that he's still alive at 138, how come no one knows."

"How come you didn't think it? How come you didn't question it?"

Marshall sat quietly. He had no answer.

"Marshall, what would happen to you if you said aloud that the president is dead anywhere near Skeyelink."

"I suspect I'd be erased in a matter of days."

"Hours, Marshall. This is their most closely guarded secret. Top priority on their surveillance. If anyone says anything like that, they'll be gone before the sun goes down. You know full well that you can't say things like that. And so everyone censors their speech. The interesting thing about self-censorship is this: once we start being careful what we say, we start being careful what we think. It's human nature. The fear of speech extends to fear of thought. Once they have that, that censorship of thought, then it's over. They've won. And it's why you never questioned it all your life."

Marshall sat and digested for a moment. "So then who is the president?"

"There's a few people calling the shots. Mylnere, for one. But mostly the last remaining trillionaires in the country."

"Trillionaires?"

"Follow the money, as they say."

"So...what does this mean?"

"All of this was built on lies. The first lie was that the HAP was a good, intelligent, successful businessman who knew what was best for the country and would fight for ordinary Americans. None of those things were true. He was a morally depraved, ignorant narcissist who bankrupted most of his business ventures and only looked out for the super wealthy. But that didn't matter, because his followers fell for his scam. And those in power around him knew that he was the only one that could hold it all together. For some reason, his followers believed him and him alone. They realized that without him, the lies would be revealed. So they made a plan to make sure he could never die."

"So what happened when he died?"

"No one was told. It was said for security reasons, he would only make appearances through hologram moving forward."

"What? This.."

"I know. It's hard having your world completely turned upside down over and over again, isn't it?"

"So...what do we do with this?"

"We tell everyone."

"How?"

"The only way to reach every American at the same time: Facts."

"Facts? You're going to tell people on Facts?"

"Yes."

"How, exactly, are you going to get them to put this on Facts?"

"We're going to ask politely," Charlotte smiled.

"Right..."

"Like everything else in our government, Facts is centralized in one place. The Market. The 52nd through 54th floors to be exact. Everything posted to Facts comes from there."

"So you're going to go up to the 52nd floor of The Market and ask them to tell everyone that the Holy American President is dead."

"Yes. With guns."

"There must be a small army of HALE agents in and around that building. You'll never get in!"

"Well, we'll have to give them something to do, won't we?"

"What do you mean?"

"What would happen if there's simultaneous explosions all over the city?"

"I...I guess they'd send out HALE agents..."

"Exactly. Almost all of them."

"So you're going to blow up the city? People are going to die."

"The buildings we're blowing have already been cleared out."

"I...but...okay. Okay, let's say this works, and you get up to the 52nd or 53rd or 54th floor. And let's say they do as you ask and tell people he's dead. No one will believe you."

"You're right. They won't. That's why we had to wait until now. But we have proof now. He had a funeral. A small, intimate one. And we finally have the video of it."

"So you're going to broadcast the video?"

"Exactly."

"And then what?"

"Well, then it's up to the people. Most Americans don't want to live under this tyranny. They're just looking for an excuse to rise up against it. We're going to give them that excuse. Even the HALE agents think they're working for the HAP. What will they do when they find out they've been lied to all this time?"

"And this will work?"

"We shall see. It's the best we can do right now. The HAP, figuratively, has been lying to the American people for decades. And they haven't had any way to check those lies for years. His lies have become the reality for most Americans. At the end of the day, it's not up to us what happens to this country. It's up to the people. All we can do is tell the truth, and hopefully they'll decide on their own. But at the very least, if this works, we'll show that there are cracks in their armor. That they're not all powerful. That people can fight back. If a video of the HAP's funeral shows up on every single American's phone at once, how can they possibly spin that for anything except a complete and utter security failure on their part. At the very least, people will know they're vulnerable. Sometimes, that's all people need: a glimmer of hope that tyranny can be overthrown."

Marshall was stunned.

At that moment, Jacob and Rosie, two of the kitchen staff, walked in, weary eyed. They silently walked over to the coffee maker and got a pot going.

"Come on," Charlotte said with a wink. "People will be hungry. Time to get to work."

Marshall got a cup of coffee, which was not as good as Eric's, but was much better than the slop he drank most of his life. The kitchen slowly filled up over the next half hour as the rest of the staff filed in. Breakfast was French toast, sausages, and scrambled eggs this morning. Marshall helped with the scrambled eggs at first and then helped the rest of the staff prep for lunch and dinner. Aside from Charlotte's minimal instructions, the kitchen was quiet and somber.

The next few hours went by quickly for Marshall. Whether it was the exhaustion from not sleeping, or his mind's long-standing ability to detach from the pain of the current moment, or his brain trying to comprehend what Charlotte shared with him, Marshall suddenly found that breakfast was done and all the prep work for the next two meals was completed. He looked up at the clock and saw that it was almost ten in the morning. Clean up had just finished and the rest of the staff filed out.

Marshall had more questions about the upcoming operation. He also had the urge to go back to The Library, the last place he spent time with Eric. He stayed, waiting until everyone else left, hoping to talk to Charlotte alone, since she was always the last one to leave the kitchen. Charlotte looked as though she was about to pass out on the counter. Marshall walked over to her and quietly asked, "I have more questions. Can you take me to The Library so we can talk? We have a few hours before lunch."

She looked at him for a moment and he thought she was going to say no. But then a sad smile cracked her lips and she nodded. "Sure, we can go for a few."

They walked out of the kitchen and towards the main door to The Nest, but just as they were about to reach it, the door opened and Marlene walked through. Marshall took one look at her face and could tell immediately that something was wrong. So could Charlotte.

"What's happened?" Charlotte asked.

"Public immolation," Marlene whispered.

"WHAT? WHEN?"

"Today. Noon."

"You can't be serious. Today? It's been only a day and they're already executing him?"

"Seems that way. Come on, we have to go."

"Go? Where are we going?" Marshall asked.

"The White House."

Charlotte grabbed Marlene's arm as he turned to leave. "Wait, Marlene. Why would they execute him so quickly?"

"I don't know. Does it matter? We have to…"

"You do know, Marlene. He's either already told them everything and they don't need him anymore, or they don't think they're getting anything out of him and are using him as bait. Which one do you think it is?"

"Dad would never tell."

"Right. I agree. So we can't go. It's exactly what they want us to do. They'll be looking for us."

"They don't know who we are!"

"We don't know that for sure."

"Well we don't know for sure if dad told them anything. We have to go and find out, don't we?"

Charlotte hesitated.

"IT'S MY FUCKING DAD, CHARLOTTE"

Charlotte nodded. "Right. Then I'm coming with you."

Marlene turned and started walking towards the front entrance and Charlotte followed suit. Marshall began walking with them. Marlene suddenly turned.

"Where do you think you're going?" she asked, staring Marshall in the eyes.

"It's Eric. He's...he's...I'm coming with you," Marshall responded. "For all I know, this is my fault. I...I have to go. I have to see him again."

Marlene opened her mouth to argue, but Charlotte softly placed a hand on her shoulder.

"Let's go. We don't have time to debate this," Charlotte said.

Marlene stared at Charlotte for a second, then back at Marshall, her eyes full of fury. Marshall sensed that Marlene was itching for a fight. But then her shoulders slumped and her eyes softened.

"Okay," she whispered. "Let's go."

16

By the time the three of them got to Constitution Avenue, there were already crowds of people heading towards The Ellipse. There had not been a public immolation in Washington DC in several months, and there was a clear excitement in the air when Marshall, Marlene, and Charlotte arrived.

The sky was overcast with dark clouds and the possibility of rain could be tasted in the air. But no amount of rain would keep people from a public immolation.

Marshall had not been to a public immolation since his time in the PCRF. It was common for children over the age of eight in the care of the Holy American President to attend, when they were lucky enough to be drawn in the lottery. Getting out of the PCRF for any event was reason for joyous celebration, Marshall had thought the first time his name was drawn to attend a public immolation. But after a few, he began wishing not to win this particular lottery.

The last time he went to one was his last year in the PCRF, when he was eighteen. He recalled the yelling and screaming as the crowd was brought up to a frothing fervor by the HAP. There were two people burned alive that day. Like all the people who were sentenced to public immolation, they were found guilty of treason against the country. Those particular two were narcoterrorists, people who waged war against America by sneaking drugs into the country in order to murder Americans through overdoses. Marshall remembered being ushered near the front of the crowd, as there was always a space there designated for PCRF children so they could have a clear view. It was important for Americans to bask in the justice of the Holy American President at an early age.

He remembered standing there, amongst a sea of expectant faces, just a few rows away from the stage, where he could clearly see the sun-kissed, olive toned faces of the two men in the glass cage, both of whom appeared to be in their fifties or early sixties. One of them appeared terrified and was crying. Marshall could see a dark stain form in the crotch of his orange prison jumpsuit. He was being held up by the other man, who was standing tall. As the crowd jeered, Marshall could see the calmer man whispering things into the other man's ear. Marshall got the distinct impression that he was trying to soothe him affectionately. But that could not be the case, as these were murderous vermin who had no sympathy for human life. An act of compassion as the one he thought he was seeing was beyond their evil minds' capabilities.

They were left there in that glass cage for what seemed like an hour to Marshall's eighteen year old mind, but looking back he now thought it was probably only a few minutes before the Holy American President spoke to the crowd. He listed their crimes and reassured the crowd that he had personally seen the evidence and that their guilt was irrefutable. He then talked at length about his love for the crowd, of the goodness of his heart, his superhuman ability to distinguish right from wrong, and several other topics regarding his own personal triumphs that Marshall at this point could no longer remember. Near the end, he told the crowd that his only desire was to keep real Americans safe from the cockroaches that try to infest this great country. Marshall distinctly remembered him pointing to the two men in the glass cage when he used the word "cockroaches." He remembered feeling like the men in that glass box did not look like cockroaches, or murderers. But he had to trust in the President because the President was always right.

This time is different, Marshall thought. *This time, I know the man in the glass cage is not going to be a murderer, or vermin, or a terrorist. Or perhaps this time isn't different. Perhaps they were never murderers, vermin, or terrorists. Perhaps the Holy American President was not always right. Perhaps he was mistaken. Or perhaps...perhaps the president is a liar.*

The thought stuck with Marshall as they wove their way through the outer edges of the crowd, which was not so densely packed.

A public immolation was one of the few occasions when one could see people of all races gather in a single place. But even so, Marlene discreetly walked a few paces ahead, while Charlotte and Marshall followed behind as inconspicuously as possible, trying to make it appear as though they were not together. Two white people walking together with a light skinned black person could easily pique the interest of the myriad HALE agents that were stationed throughout the area.

As they made their way down Constitution Ave, past 10th, 12th, and 14th streets, the crowd began to grow heavier. By the time they hit 15th street, it started to become difficult to find space between the people. But Marlene was relentless and continued to force her way through. Marshall would not have been able to follow her had he not been with Charlotte, who plowed through ahead of him, creating a lane for him to follow.

After a few minutes, they found themselves at the edge of The Ellipse. The Immolation Tower was a permanent, eighteen foot tall square structure made of granite, about half the size of a tennis court. The top half of the stone structure was adorned with large screens, on which the immolation would be projected for everyone to see. Speakers were attached to each corner, both for the Holy American President's address, which he always gave before each immolation, and so the crowd could hear the screams of the criminal in the cage—even though they claimed the process was instantaneous and painlessly humane.

Atop the stone sat a glass cage, inset from the edge about two feet. This was called the Fire Box.

When they were about twenty yards from the Tower, the crowd began to tighten, as if it were one unified organism, and Marlene could no longer push through. Charlotte squeezed up next to her and Marshall came up between the two. From there they had a relatively clear view of the tower. The Fire Box was empty.

Marshall looked around at the endless faces, most of which were looking down at their phones. A few expectant faces stared up at the tower.

"Remember, they're watching," Marlene said quietly.

Marshall nodded. A few seconds later he realized he was not sure what that really meant, so he asked. "What does that mean?"

"We need to act like the rest of the crowd."

"Okay," Marshall responded, still not quite sure what to do. He figured he would simply go along with whatever Marlene and Charlotte did. He scanned the crowd again, wondering how many other people here were from The Resistance. How many people knew Eric.

Suddenly the speakers kicked on and he could hear a slight static emanating from them. A moment later, a realistic hologram of the Holy American President appeared at each corner of the tower. He wore a blue gray suit, a white collared shirt, and a red tie. His hair was coiffed to the side as usual. If there were not four of him on the Tower, the holograms individually could easily be mistaken as the real thing.

"Hello, my fellow Americans," his voice boomed over the speakers.

The crowd cheered. Marshall saw Marlene and Charlotte cheer as well, and he joined in a half second later. At first, he felt awkward in doing so. But after a moment, years of feigning enthusiasm at work kicked in and he became one of the crowd. The Holy American President stood waving and smiling. He was known for loving the applause and adulation of his supporters and would stand there for as long as they would grant him this flattery. And so Marshall, Marlene, and Charlotte continued to clap and cheer for the HAP, who was about to murder a man the three of them loved dearly.

After a few minutes the cheering died down organically and the Holy American President began.

"It's such a lovely day today, isn't it? So lovely. A beautiful day for JUSTICE!"

The crowd once again erupted in applause.

"We don't do these enough, do we? We got to be tough. The lunatics on the other side will never quit, and so can't we. We got to be tough and show them we'll always win. AMERICA WILL ALWAYS WIN!"

Another eruption. After a few minutes the crowd quieted down again. Then, in the middle of the glass cage, Marshall watched in horror as Eric slowly appeared as a platform from within the tower brought him to the surface. He was wearing a bright orange jumpsuit that looked to be clean and brand new. His body was hunched over and listed to the right, and it was clear he was having difficulty holding himself up. His left eye was swollen shut and black and blue. There was a distinct cut that ran from the right side of his lip up his cheek. He held his left arm in his right as if he were protecting it. Eric looked out over the crowd slowly with his right eye.

Marshall gasped, and then felt Marlene's hand grab his, forcefully squeezing it as a reminder to mimic the angry crowd. He expected Marlene to release his hand immediately but she did not. The skin of her hand was not smooth by any means, and he could feel the callouses and ridges of hard work; yet holding her hand was soothing. He swallowed hard.

The crowd erupted again, but this time in angry yelling and booing and hissing.

"FUCKING TERRORIST!"

"PIECE OF SHIT!"

"TRAITOR TO YOUR RACE!"

And finally the crowd unified under one chant: "BURN HIM! BURN HIM! BURN HIM!" as they pumped their fist in the air in unison. Marshall reluctantly joined in, pumping the fist of his free hand, as Marlene and Charlotte did the same.

Marshall's chest tingled with rage and sadness. At the same time he felt a giddy excitement as Marlene continued to hold his hand, and consequently shame at feeling even an ounce of joy in this moment.

That is when the Holy American President's tirade began. He yelled about the domestic terrorists who continued to poison the minds and blood of innocent young Americans. The Holy American President spoke for a half hour about how the murderers, rapists, and animals from shithole countries continue to invade America. The country would be overrun with these people, who are the worst of the worst, if it were not for him. Him, and him alone was the only thing standing in the way of the country failing and turning into another one of these shithole countries.

Eric stood there quietly as the President railed against enemies of the state and his own personal enemies, then touted his own personal triumphs, and his own personal accolades. Marshall could tell Eric was in pain, that standing was excruciating. But Eric would not sit, would not lie down. He just stood there, shaking slightly, but clearly unwilling to give into the pain in his last moments. The cameras zoomed in on his battered face, projected onto the huge screens at the top of the stone tower, and Marshall could see defiance in his eye.

The sound of the Holy American President's voice droned on for several more minutes, but Marshall did not hear anymore of his words. He had heard all of the president's gripes and self-congratulatory talk before and this speech was no different.

Finally, after what felt like hours, the Holy American President stopped talking, and the crowd erupted again, chanting "BURN HIM! BURN HIM!"

"You ready for an IMMOLATION?" The president said, exaggerating the last word into several syllables.

The crowd cheered. Marshall, Marlene, and Charlotte cheered along with them.

Marshall watched as Eric slowly lifted his right hand up, and placed his pointer finger to his lips, and smiled ever so slightly. Then the entire Fire Box was engulfed in flames. Usually, the screams of those in the Fire Box could be heard from the speakers, but this time there was only silence. Eric had not uttered a sound.

17

It took about half an hour for the crowd to unpack itself from The Ellipse. The chatter around Marshall, Marlene, and Charlotte ranged from jubilant and celebratory to quiet and tired. But Marshall did not hear one word of concern for Eric, questions about who he was, or what he had done to deserve his fate.

By the time they had reached 10th avenue, it had begun to rain. The rain began as a drizzle, but within a few minutes the sky had opened up and the rain was coming down in sheets, drenching the crowd. Some people had umbrellas, but even they got completely soaked. Most people ran for shelter but Marlene, Marshall, and Charlotte walked steadily forward, Marlene about twenty yards ahead of the other two.

The coolness of the water was refreshing for Marshall after the suffocating heat generated by the thousands of spectators, packed into a confined space, on that humid, March day. As the rain came down even harder. Marshall's ears flooded with the sound of the incessant beating that the ground was taking from the rain. The large raindrops began to feel like miniscule marbles falling in droves. But even the pain of the torrent was relieving, as it distracted Marshall from the pain of losing his friend. It occurred to Marshall that the sky was crying, and in that moment he realized that he was as well.

Within minutes, the streets were flooded and the crowd had largely dispersed, searching for shelter. Marlene walked on, trudging through the ankle deep water, undaunted by the bitter downpour, and Charlotte and Marshall had no choice but to follow on, keeping at as far a distance as possible while still being able to see her through the punishing deluge.

It took over an hour to get past the freeway. Once there, Marshall thought it would be safer to walk together, and wanted to catch up with Marlene, who at that point was over a hundred yards ahead of them. But as he was about to start jogging towards her, he felt Charlotte grip his arm firmly.

"She just watched her father burned alive. If she wants company, she'll wait for us. Otherwise, give her her space," Charlotte said loudly over the sound of the heavy rain hitting the earth.

Marshall nodded and slowed down. Marlene did not.

The image of Eric in the firebox popped into Marshall's mind.

"Why did Eric put his finger to his lips in the firebox?" Marshall asked.

"He knew we would be out there, watching. It was a sign. A signal. He didn't tell them anything. Not a word."

"He's tougher than I'd ever imagined…"

"Eric? Tough doesn't begin to describe that man."

They walked on for another forty-five minutes before they reached the safe house that they had exited the tunnels from originally. It was a small, unassuming two story house at a t-intersection that looked over all of 13th street, which the three of them were walking down. Marshall watched through the rain as Marlene, still over a hundred yards away, reached the house first, climbed a few steps up to the porch, and opened the door.

Marshall and Charlotte never saw or heard them coming. At the next intersection a black sedan pulled in front of them and three masked men with large automatic weapons jumped out of the car. Marshall and Charlotte immediately turned to run, only to find a phalanx of masked HALE agents behind them, guns drawn.

Marshall turned to Charlotte, hoping she would have a solution, a way out. She looked at him and at that moment he saw deep sadness behind her eyes.

"Goodbye, Marshall," she said quietly.

She smiled briefly and then reached her hand into her coat as if to pull something out of her pocket. The world exploded with gunfire and Charlotte fell to the ground. Marshall stood, stunned, and looked down at Charlotte's lifeless body as blood seeped onto the rain-soaked sidewalk, mixing with the water in paisley like swirls. Her empty hands lay beside her.

There was shouting all around him but it sounded muffled, as if they were yelling into pillows. All he could really hear was his heart pounding in his chest. An acrid, sulfurous smell, which Marshall assumed was from the gunfire, wafted into his nose, mixing with the smell of wet concrete.

Marshall turned back around to see men running towards Marlene, who was standing on the stoop of the safehouse. A moment later, she was gone, the door closed behind her.

A sharp pain suddenly exploded behind Marshall's left knee and it buckled beneath him, collapsing him to the ground. He felt a knee on his back as his arms were aggressively pulled behind him. He thought his shoulders were about to pop out of their sockets as they zip tied his hands together.

He looked up to see if he could see Marlene, yet at the same time knowing full well she was gone and he would probably never see her again. He watched the HALE agents approach the house and begin climbing the stairs. Just before the black bag was slipped over his head, Marshall saw the house erupt into flames. His ears popped with the sound of the explosion. The HALE agents at the front door disappeared in the fireball.

And then everything was black.

18

Marshall regained consciousness in a chair. At first he thought it was night time, or that he was in a dark room, but quickly realized his head was still in the black bag. The air in the bag was musty and he could smell the tinny aroma of blood, which he assumed was his own. Slowly he began to take stock of his body. The first thing he noticed was that his hands were bound to the sides of the chair. He felt a sharp pain in his stomach where he had been punched and the back of his head was throbbing.

He could feel a heat against the skin of his chest and legs, which was emanating from a source directly in front of him. This heat in front of him was in direct contrast to the icy metallic chair he was sitting in, which felt so cold it almost burned his skin.

And it was at that moment he realized with horror that aside from the bag on his head, he was naked.

He tried to move his arms but they were securely strapped to the chair with a rough, prickly rope. His ankles were similarly strapped to the front legs of the chair. He tried to stand up, thinking he could lift the chair, but the chair appeared to be secured to the floor.

Panic set in and it suddenly became extremely difficult to breath in the bag.

"HELP!" Marshall yelled. "LET ME OUT OF HERE! LET ME OUT OF HERE! I CAN'T BREATH! LET ME OUT OF HERE!" His voice sounded stifled within the bag, as if the whole world was contained in the space between his face and the cloth. The universe beyond the bag answered with silence.

Marshall began thrashing his body, hoping somehow he'd break loose but at the same time knowing it was hopeless. The throbbing in his head intensified and he stopped moving for a second, trying to catch his breath beneath the cloth bag. He tried to calm his body, taking deep breaths, but it did not work.

"LET ME GO! I DIDN'T DO ANYTHING! LET ME THE FUCK OUT OF HERE!"

He closed his eyes and then opened them again. It made no difference. The darkness within the bag was complete. He focused all of his energy on his right arm and with a sudden yank, pulled it with all his strength. It did not make a difference. His arm did not budge an inch.

"PLEASE! PLEASE! SOMEONE HELP ME! LET ME GO!"

There was no answer. He sat quietly, thinking through the last day. Suddenly his mouth felt parched. His tongue felt like sandpaper against the roof of his mouth. And his stomach growled with hunger. He wondered how long he had been out for. How long had he been sitting in that chair, naked, and unconscious. How long since the last time he drank anything or ate anything. There was no way to tell. He could not even tell how long it had been since he had woken up in that chair. Has it been a few minutes? Hours? His head throbbed at the thought.

Surely they won't just let me starve to death on this chair right? I'd die of thirst first anyway. But what would be the point of that? Easier to just shoot me. Less painful though. That's probably the point. Punishment.

He thought back to Eric in the firebox and envied him at that moment. *At least that would be quick. Sitting here until I die...I can't believe this is how it's going to end.*

Then he thought about Marlene. He would never see her again. She probably did not even know where he was. Would she wonder about him? Would she miss him? At this thought, he began to cry. At first it was a whimper, and then his chest began heaving. He could feel the mucus from his nose dripping onto the cloth of the black bag, and then rubbing against the skin of his nose and his cheeks as his head nodded uncontrollably with each sob.

"Pathetic," came a calm, sanctimonious voice from in front of him.

Marshall picked his head up instinctually, looking for the source of the voice, but all he could see was blackness.

"He-he-hello?" Marshall stuttered through his tears.

"You should see yourself, Marshall Smith. You look pathetic."

"Who, who is that? Who are you?" Marshall asked. Suddenly the black bag was ripped from his head. A bright spotlight was shining directly at him and he was immediately blinded by it. He closed his eyes, tilted his head to the side away from the light, and opened his eyes to try to help them adjust. Slowly his vision came back.

Marshall looked around. He was in a small concrete room. To his left and right were bare walls. He tried to look behind him to see who took off the black hood, but he didn't see anyone. The light in front of him was large and the space behind it was in complete shadow.

"When's the attack, Marshall?" the voice from the darkness asked.

Marshall did not remember hearing anyone come into the room and wondered if the speaker had been in here the entire time, watching him. He looked down at his own body and saw that he was covered in sweat, grime, and bruises.

He strained his eyes to see beyond the light and find the person behind it, but could not make out anything.

"When's the attack, Marshall?" the voice repeated.

"I...I don't know anything."

"You're lying, Marshall."

"I...I don't know."

"When's the attack, Marshall?"

"Really, I don't know."

"Marshall, we're going to hurt you if you don't tell us, you know that don't you?" The voice said calmly.

"I...I really don't know, please, please," Marshall began to feel tears streaming down his face.

Marshall almost wished the man behind the light would scream at him or swear at him. The calmness of the man's voice as he threatened him was unnerving.

"We know you've been in contact with The Resistance. We know you knew Eric Blair. We know a lot of things, Marshall. And so we know when you're lying."

"I...I...I don't know anything about an attack."

"Tell me about Eric."

"Eh..e..Eric? I...he...I don't know an Eric."

The man behind the spotlight sighed. "You're not a very good liar, Marshall. And I don't have much patience for liars."

Suddenly, a blinding pain coursed through Marshall's body. Every muscle tensed and froze and his eyes felt like bursting. His back and hamstrings erupted as if they were on fire. The air left his body and his lungs were frozen, unable to draw in more. Even his thoughts were frozen, as the only thing his mind could comprehend was the agony pumping through him. And then it was gone.

"The chair is electrified," the voice explained calmly. "That was just a taste. I can leave it on for longer. I can turn up the voltage. I don't have to though, if you just tell me the truth."

Marshall's entire body wilted and his lungs heaved as he tried to catch his breath. He smelled something pungent and acrid in the air and quickly realized it was his own skin that was touching the chair.

"Please...please...I...I don't really know anything. Really."

The pain lasted longer this time. It felt like several minutes, but as soon as it was done he knew it had only been for a few seconds. When it stopped, the smell was more potent and nauseating. The skin on his back and on the back of his legs stung. Marshall felt drool dripping down his chin and tasted iron in his mouth. Then he realized the drool was actually blood, and he had bit his own tongue.

"Marshall, we know you know Eric. And we know he was in The Resistance. Do you want to know how we know? We found your phone, Marshall. The one under the sink? You remember that phone? Wasn't the best hiding place, Marshall. 'There is something wrong with this world. Something terrible, awful, inhumane. Of all the people I've ever met, am I the only one to see it? Well, me and Mr. Blaire that is.' Do you remember writing that, Marshall? I guess we should thank you for that. You led us right to him."

"YOU MURDERED HIM!" Marshall screamed as best he could as the blood from his bitten tongue filled his mouth.

"One might argue you did, Marshall."

"No...that's not true. You did it," Marshall whimpered. But he was not sure of that.

"Your own stupidity led us to him, Marshall. And your own stupidity will lead us to the rest of them. Now, tell us what you know. Where is their base?"

"I...I really don't know. I don't know how to get there."

"So...the base does exist? And you admit you've been there then?"

Marshall fell silent. His mind tried to sift through the information he was just given. *They don't know about The Nest. Not definitively. Marlene. I already gave up Eric. I can't give up Marlene. No matter what, I won't give them anything. I don't care what they do to me. I won't talk. We're all dead anyway.*

"I don't like waiting, Marshall," the voice said. Marshall's muscles seized again. His flesh tingled. His teeth bit against themselves so hard he thought they might shatter like glass. And then it was gone.

There was silence as Marshall tried to catch his breath. He turned his head and spit out a glob of blood onto the floor. He tried to focus his mind past the pain. He lifted his head to look past the light, but still could not see anything.

After a few more moments, the voice asked, "Where's the base, Marshall?"

Marshall stared into the darkness. "I...I don't know what you're talking about," Marshall answered, determinately.

"Wrong answer, Marshall."

"At least let me see who I'm talking to," Marshall said quickly, before the man behind the light could turn the chair back on.

"You think knowing who I am will help you? Marshall, you're never getting out of here alive. The only thing you have left to do in your life is to tell us what you know."

"WHO ARE YOU?" Marshall screamed.

"Fine, you want to know? This is the last face you'll ever see." At that the spotlight shut off and overhead lights in front of Marshall flickered on. Behind the spotlight stood a gray, metal desk, behind which sat a gaunt, stern faced, balding man with vampiric pale skin in a navy blue suit, light blue collared shirt, and red tie. His eyes flickered with an intensity that can only stem from unspeakable hatred. Mylnere: the Holy American President's chief advisor and the head of HALE. Marshall had seen his weekly address for years. In them, he always looked like someone not to be trifled with. And it was well known that he was ruthless and unapologetic when it came to his policies. He would order the torture or execution of anyone without hesitation.

So looking at him now, small, frail, with the tininess of his beady eyes emphasized by his abnormally large forehead that appeared to continue infinitely into the pale bald skin of his scalp, Marshall could not help but laugh, despite the pain.

Mylnere stood up in a rush, causing his chair to topple over behind him. "WHAT THE FUCK ARE YOU LAUGHING ABOUT?" he yelled, suddenly losing the eerie calmness in his voice.

Marshall spit again, this time towards Mylnere. His blood splattered on the floor in front of him. "You, Mylnere," Marshall said quietly. "You try to pretend you're this big, tough guy. But I see you for what you really are." Marshall could see Mylnere's face and bald head redden and his fists clench as he tried to contain his anger. "You're a sad, pathetic little man," Marshall continued. "And you'll never win."

Mylnere opened his mouth, about to respond, but then appeared to think better of it. He took a breath, straightened his tie and pulled his suit jacket down. He then walked around the grey desk in front of him, upon which sat a singular dial that Marshall assumed controlled the voltage of the chair he sat in. Mylnere took a few steps towards Marshall until he stood over him. Marshall braced himself as Mylnere clenched his fist and swung. The punch landed a glancing blow off the side of Marshall's head. Mylnere shook his hand out, and it was evident to Marshall that the punch hurt Mylnere's hand more than it did Marshall's head.

"I already won," Mylnere said, in as stern a voice as he could muster. "You'll talk. You'll talk, and then you'll die, and then all your friends will die."

"We're all dead anyway," Marshall responded.

Mylnere's eyes flashed with distasteful recognition. *He's heard that before. I wonder if Eric said the same thing to him.*

Mylnere forced a smile. "Some time in the cell and you'll talk. I'll be seeing you soon."

With that, Mylnere stepped behind the spotlight. A gray door, which blended in with the concrete, stood behind the desk. Mylnere walked out of the door, leaving Marshall alone in the room. Or so he thought.

A moment later, the black bag was forcefully shoved over his head again. He never saw the blow coming.

19

Marshall woke up in a heap on a hard, frigid concrete floor. His naked body ached. He tried stretching out his legs, but all his muscles groaned at the effort. He slowly rolled over onto his back, which immediately felt like it was being stabbed by a thousand needles. But almost as quickly as the agony hit, the cool floor soothed the pain until it dulled away.

He took a deep breath, trying to check in with the rest of his body. Each sense seemed to come on individually. Aside from the coolness of the floor, he could feel the cold air around him, and a steady breeze coming from above. He suddenly began shivering, as if his body was waiting for his brain to acknowledge the cold. He took another deep breath through his nose. The air was completely odorless. The room was also silent, except for the faint sound of the cold air slipping invisibly through a vent into the room.

Lastly, his vision, which was blurred at first, slowly returned. He looked around. Another concrete room. Above him, he could see a square white vent, from which he assumed the cold air was coming from. Around the vent were 4 bright, circular, inset lights, which were blinding when he looked directly at them. The room was just large enough for his hands and feet to be able to touch the opposite walls at the same time. He reached above his head with his hands and felt the concrete wall, which, like the floor, was cold to the touch. There was a solid metal door, painted white, to his left. To his right was a metal toilet sticking out from the wall in one corner, and what appeared to be a large piece of aluminum foil folded up in the other corner.

Seeing the toilet made him realize he had to urinate. He got up gingerly and staggered over to the toilet, each step an agony for his muscles. When he reached the toilet, rather than peeing, he immediately vomited. There did not seem to be much in his stomach, as it was mostly bile. The room immediately smelled sour and rancid. He vomited again. Marshall looked at his own sickness in the toilet and began to feel sick again. He flushed the toilet, hoping to get rid of the smell, and then slid down to the floor. His back began hurting again, and he leaned against the cold concrete wall to ease the pain.

After a few seconds he began to shiver again. Had he had clothes on, the temperature may have been tolerable. He looked back at the shiny object in the opposite corner. With extreme effort, Marshall crawled over to the object. It was a thin, metallic sheet that Marshall decided must be some sort of blanket. It crinkled when he opened it up. He placed it over himself, hoping it would retain some of his body heat.

It was at that moment that he noticed a small, square hole in the wall which he had been leaning against a moment ago. He slowly got up, wrapped the sheet around him and took a few steps over to it. The sheet crinkled with every movement.

The hole was at eye level and slightly smaller than his head. He looked in and saw a shaft. He could not tell how long the shaft was but at the end he could see the light blue sky and a whiff of a cloud, which was drifting by. *What is the purpose of this?* No answer popped into his head. All he knew was he yearned to climb out of that shaft. It seemed clear that he was not at ground level, and he could not be sure how many floors up he was. But he would give up anything to be able to shrink down in size, run down the shaft, and jump out of the hole at the end of it. That was when he realized the purpose. *Hope, freedom, or even death is at the other end of this shaft. I can see it, but I can't reach it. It's here to remind me that there's a world outside of this room that I'll never see again.*

He slid back down to the floor, wrapped the sheet around him, curled up into a ball, and started to cry.

* * *

When he awoke the room was the same except for two things. The lights were dimmed and there was a tray near the door.

Marshall crawled out from under the metallic sheet and over to it. A standard food ration. He peeled off the top and stared at the meal: four cubes of what appeared to be some sort of protein-based substitute for meat, a green paste, a dry piece of bread, and a small sealed plastic cup of water. There were no utensils. Marshall quickly drank the water, realizing how thirsty he was, and then used his hands to shovel every morsel down eagerly. He had no idea how long it had been since he had eaten. There was barely any taste to any of it. Marshall licked his fingers clean.

As soon as he finished, a small, four-inch-tall opening, which had been well camouflaged, slid open at the bottom of the door. He looked at it for a second and immediately realized what he was supposed to do and slid the tray under it. The opening slid shut and the door was whole again.

So they're watching me. Marshall thought. *Of course they are.* He looked around but did not see any cameras.

Marshall then stood up gingerly and went over to the hole in the wall. The sky was a dark navy blue, there were no stars, and just a little moonlight. Marshall sat back down.

He stared around the room again. Nothing had changed.

Marshall shivered. He pulled up the metallic sheet and covered himself back up.

He sat, staring at the wall opposite him for several minutes. His back still hurt. The whisper of the cold air flowing into the cell continued at a steady pace.

I wonder if Marlene is alive. I hope she made it out. If she died, it was because she went to Eric's immolation. He was caught because of me. Because of my carelessness. And if she's dead too, then that would be my fault as well, wouldn't it? But I didn't know. I didn't understand. It can't be my fault. It can't be my fault because...

The dim lights suddenly flashed on to bright white, and the cell was bathed in brightness. Marshall instinctively raised his hand to his eyes to shield them from the light. As soon as his eyes readjusted, he looked around the cell.

Nothing else had changed.

He got up slowly and looked out of the hole in the wall, and could see the sky was brightening. *It must be morning. I wonder how long ago they caught me. But at least I know I've only been in this cell for about a day.*

He sat back down. The concrete was cold against his bare buttocks.

Charlotte. They killed Charlotte! Didn't even give her a chance. Why did she have to reach for her pocket? She must have known. She did it on purpose. She knew they would shoot. She didn't want to end up in a cell like this. Like me. She must have known. We're all dead anyway. Eric's dead. Charlotte is dead. I'm next. No matter what they do to me, I can't tell them anything.

He sat quietly for some time. His buttocks began to fall asleep. He tried shifting positions but there was no way to be comfortable. He stood up and paced the cell slowly. He counted how many times he could pace around the cell, trying to occupy his time. He knew they were watching, and did not want to give them the satisfaction of asking for help, or begging, or any communication at all.

They're hoping to wait me out, well I can wait them out. They won't get anything from me.

He got to twenty-two before his legs started to give out. The back of this left knee pained him from when he was hit there however many days ago it was.

The small opening at the base of the door slid open and another standard food ration slid through. *Must be close to noontime.* He opened it up. Inside was the same meal he had at breakfast. At first he did not want to eat, but hunger overpowered his will and he methodically chewed the food and swallowed it until it was gone. The slit opened up and Marshall slid the empty food ration back through.

He stood up and walked over to the hole in the wall. It was a bright day outside. He stuck his nose in the hole but the smell was no different. *Maybe it's farther than it looks.* He reached his arm into the hole up to his armpit to see if he could get a better sense of how far the free sky was, but it made no difference. It was impossibly far away.

Marshall lay down on his side, pulled the metallic sheet over his body and rested his head against his arm.

This is it. This is the rest of my life. No one is coming for me.

He got up and began pacing again, but by the fourteenth time his legs grew weary again. He tried to maintain his focus and push through. He gave himself a goal of twenty but ended up sitting in the corner after only one more time around. He slunk back down to the ground and listened to the air being pushed into the room.

He looked around. The cell was the same.

If only I had just kept walking. If I didn't step into that damn antique store. I'd be…I'd be at my desk right now, erasing people from history. Erasing people from their mothers, from their fathers, from their friends.

He looked around the cell again.

I'd rather be here, he thought, determinedly.

He closed his eyes. He did not feel tired, but that did not matter. There was nothing else to do. Marshall fell asleep quickly.

* * *

Thirteen times the lights dimmed and then brightened. Thirty nine standard ration meals, all containing the exact same food were slid into the cell, eaten, and slid back out. Marshall paced, and ate. He looked out of the hole in the wall at the freedom that was beyond his reach. His mind slowly began melting away into itself. And he slept.

* * *

Marshall was at the antique store. Except it was not an antique store. Instead of knickknacks and tchotchkes, the shelves were filled with books. The bookcases towered over Marshall and extended seemingly infinitely. As he looked up at the vast, ceilingless librarial expanse above him, Marshall felt crushingly small and insignificant. The feeling weighed on his chest and he had trouble breathing.

He knew he had to escape the store, but he could not see a door beyond the bookcases. He began running around, down one aisle and up another but each aisle looked exactly the same and he was not sure if he was circling back to the same spot over and over again. He tried calling out for help but no sound escaped his lips.

In an instant, without knowing how, he realized his escape was within the books themselves. He grabbed a random book off the shelf. It had a dark green leather binding that was soft to the touch. He opened it up, looking for the key to escape but immediately saw that the pages were filled with gibberish. He grabbed another book, a book with bright red binding, and opened it only to find the same. As were the third, fourth, and fifth books he pulled off the shelf. He ran to another aisle and pulled a book off the shelf. On the page he flipped to he noticed a singular complete word amongst another page of gibberish: think.

Think. Was that a clue? He opened the book to the last page, page 410. This page was the same as the others. It seemed as though every page was a random collection of letters, as if each book was typed by blind monkeys. Surely there was something here that would help him escape.

Perhaps the books above would have some meaning. He began climbing the bookcase in front of him and found he could scale it easily. Within seconds he was a thousand shelves above the floor. He looked down and could no longer see the ground. Books above him and books below. He thought that he should be afraid, but he found he was not.

Hanging there with one hand, he pulled a book off a shelf with the other and opened it. More gibberish, until one page caught his eye. On it was a simple phrase. "Two plus two makes four."

He lost his grip and fell. The book tumbled past him. He fell and fell and continued to fall until he felt like he was no longer falling, but instead was flying.

*   *   *

When Marshall awoke, the lights were dim again. He had no idea what time it was. The cell was the same. A standard food ration sat on the floor by the door.

His entire body was stiff from sleeping on the floor. He got up and slowly stretched his muscles. The pain from his burned back and buttocks had transitioned into an insufferable itch. He got up and looked out of the hole in the wall. It was pitch black outside. *Must be a new moon out there.*

He sat down next to the standard food ration and ate his dinner slowly. *No need to rush.*

After he finished, the slot slid open and he pushed the empty food ration through. The slot slid closed.

Marshall went back over to the hole and looked out, not really sure what he was looking for. It was still pitch black.

He sat back down, pulled his legs up to his chest, and pulled the metallic sheet on top of him.

He listened to the quietness of the cell. Then he heard a whispering sound coming from the corner where the toilet sat.

"Hello?" he said. His voice was gruff and guttural. He cleared his throat.

"Hello," he said more definitely. There was no response.

"HELLO!" he yelled. His voice echoed off the walls for a second and then was gone.

The sound was gone. He listened for a while, sure that there was someone there. Maybe behind the wall. He listened intently.

They have to come get me at some point. They have questions they want answered. How long can they leave me in here for?

He looked around the cell. It was the same.

"Keep it together, Marshall," he whimpered to himself.

Shouldn't have said that. They're listening. They're waiting for me to crack. Don't say anything.

He got up and began pacing circles around the cell again.

Have to get to twenty-five.

After eighteen circles, he began to struggle. His body still ached. He pushed through until he reached twenty-five and then sat back down.

He looked down at his body and thought how strange it was that he had so quickly become accustomed to his own nakedness. But then he quickly covered himself up with the metallic sheet and closed his eyes.

* * *

The woman with the black curly hair sat next to Marshall on the cold, concrete floor. But it was not her. This was someone else. He looked up into her face, which was somewhat different than the one he remembered from his screen at the Agency of Historical Accuracy. This woman's face was slightly thinner, her eyes a soft hazelnut color. But the hair was the same. She wore a comfortable looking pair of gray sweatpants and a sweatshirt to match, as if she were at home on a rainy Saturday evening, getting ready to settle in for the night. She smiled at him.

"Marshall," she said softly.

Marshall sat up. She opened up her arms and he rested his head against her chest and began to cry.

"It's okay, Marshall. It's okay. I'm here. You're doing just fine."

"Mom," he said through the tears. "I'm sorry."

"Sorry for what, dear?"

"I forgot you. I erased you. I let your memory die," he sobbed.

"You did what you had to do to survive, Marshall. No one can blame you for that. But I'm back. You didn't erase me for good. You just kept me hidden away until it was safe."

Marshall nestled further into her body, seeking a refuge he had yearned for for decades. She stroked his hair gently.

* * *

He woke up in the same position. The lights were dim. He felt the tears on his face. The image of his mother lingered. For the first time in almost forty years, Marshall remembered his mother. He remembered her picking him up and carrying him around their small, two bedroom apartment. He remembered the floral dresses she liked to wear and the sweet coconut smell of her favorite shampoo. He remembered playing knights with her, using sticks as fake swords at the playground. He remembered her telling him stories at night as he tucked into the crook of her arm. He remembered the smell of fresh coffee in the morning, waking up and walking out to their kitchen where his father and mother would be sitting with a fresh cup.

His father. He remembered his father, always in the kitchen cooking, devising new ways to make their weekly allotment of food taste novel and exciting. He remembered the gold watch he always wore. He remembered taking the bus with him, calling out all the stops to the passengers as his father beamed at him. He remembered the small basketball hoop he had gotten for his birthday one year, and watching his father set it up in the living room for them to play. He remembered his mother flying in from seemingly out of nowhere as his father took a shot, blocking it and then throwing the ball to Marshall, while laughing and waving a finger at his father.

He remembered.

He remembered his mother telling him he was going to be a big brother. He remembered the small crib they brought into their bedroom. He remembered demanding the crib go in his bedroom, so he could look after his soon to be little sister. He remembered the hospital. He remembered wandering down the hall unattended, after his father had asked him to stay in the waiting room. He remembered seeing his father yelling at the doctors. He remembered his mother lying on the bed, her eyes glazed over.

He remembered his father taking him for ice cream. He remembered the strawberry. He remembered the masked men taking his father into the unmarked van.

He remembered it all.

Tears streamed down Marshall's face. His entire body heaved with every emotion imaginable. He felt immense joy at having recovered something priceless that he assumed was lost forever. With that, he felt immense sadness, reliving the loss that his brain had worked so hard to bury. And he felt incredible rage. Rage at what had happened to them. Rage at what was taken from him.

He cried and shook and cried, his mind completely unaware of his body as he struggled to comprehend all the memories that came flooding back.

He screamed into the empty cell. The echo screamed back at him.

Eventually, exhausted by his own wrath, he fell back asleep.

* * *

The lights were bright when he awoke. His body was stiff from sleeping on the hard floor again. His anger raged.

A standard ration meal sat on the floor by the door. He walked over, picked it up, and hurled it against the opposite wall.

He screamed again.

Suddenly the door opened.

Behind it was a brightly lit long hallway. Mylnere stood about six feet beyond the door, smiling.

"Had enough?"

Marshall rushed at him in a fury, ready to pummel him with his bare hands.

As soon as he stepped out of the door, a black baton swung out, landing directly on his chest. He felt his ribs crack as he crumpled to the floor. Two masked HALE agents stood on either side of the door. His head was bagged. Then he was picked by the armpits as he tried desperately to breath, and dragged down the hall with his feet trailing behind him.

After a few minutes he was sat in a chair, his arms and legs were tied to it, and the hood was removed. It was the same room as before, or at least an identical one.

Mylnere sat in front of him in a navy blue suit, white collared shirt, and gray tie. The white overhead lights reflected off his pasty bald head in little circles.

"Ready to talk?" Mylnere asked calmly.

"Fuck you," Marshall replied, equally calmly.

"No need for profanity, Marshall. We can skip all the pain and all the torture. Just tell us what you know."

"I don't know anything, and if I did, I'd never tell you."

Mylnere smiled. "We shall see about that."

He nodded to someone behind Marshall. As Marshall turned to see who was behind him, a HALE agent grabbed him by the hair. The back of the chair lurched backwards until Marshall was lying flat on his back and a cloth was placed over his face. Cold water then began pouring over the cloth, seeping into his nostrils and down his throat. Panic immediately set in as Marshall's body thrashed about trying to find oxygen, but there was only water. A searing pain flooded his nose and throat as the water stole the air from his lungs. His body tried to cough to expel the water but it could not. There was only more water. The roar of the water filled his ears. His entire world was drowning.

And then it was done. The back of the chair was sat up and the cloth removed. Marshall's body coughed and gaged. Oxygen flooded back into his lungs, but even that felt like a thousand blades attacking his airway. He then vomited all over himself.

His eyes watered and he squinted as he continued coughing. His shoulders ached as his body convulsed against the bindings that held his arms to the chair. His heart pounded. The panic continued, even though it was over, as if his mind knew he was alive but his body had yet to receive the message.

After several moments, Marshall finally regained his breath. His throat ached from coughing.

"Old, but effective, wouldn't you say?" Mylnere asked. "Now let's try this again. Where's the base?"

"Fuck you," Marshall gasped.

Mylnere nodded and Marshall found himself on his back again. This time he was sure he was going to die. His entire body felt frozen as the rush of water invaded his body. The choking feeling was all encompassing as his body once again struggled against the bindings in a desperate attempt to find the oxygen his lungs craved.

He was sat back up. His throat burned and his nostrils were on fire. The coughing seemed like it would never stop. Through his tears he saw Mylnere sitting in his chair, legs crossed, smiling at him.

"I could do this all day, Marshall. In fact, the less you talk, the more enjoyable this is for me. You see, this is my favorite part of the job. Watching animals like you suffer. But I also have other things to attend to. So why don't you just tell me what you know and you can go back to your cell."

Marshall took a few minutes to catch his breath. He tried to think of what to say. He had to say something, anything to give himself more time before the water came again. *I can tell him what they already know.*

"Okay, okay," Marshall sputtered. "Yes, I know Eric. I wandered into his store. He told me about The Resistance."

"See? Isn't that easier? Now where's the base?"

"I don't know anything about a base. He just told me he was part of it and asked me to join. That's it!"

"Bullshit. You were at the immolation with two women. A Charlotte Perkins and a Marlene Douglas. We know they're also part of The Resistance. And we know you haven't been to your apartment since the day you called in sick. So where have you been staying?"

"At the antique store."

"Strike two, Marshall. Lie to me again and you'll get the water."

At that moment, another masked HALE agent stepped into the room and whispered something into Mylnere's ear. A look of alarm briefly crossed Mylnere's face. The agent stepped out.

"It's your lucky day. There's something I have to attend to, Marshall. I hope you've enjoyed your time in the cell."

"Fuck you. It's been just fine."

"When we pulled you out today, you didn't seem just fine."

"I survived the last couple weeks. I can do a few more."

"Weeks?" Mylnere smiled. "Marshall, it's been three days."

With that, Mylnere got up and walked towards the door. "I'll see you tomorrow," he said gleefully, and left the room. The black bag was shoved back over Marshall's head.

20

The hood was ripped off of his head and he was thrown back in his cell. The door slammed shut with a loud bang. He looked around. The cell was the same. The standard ration meal that he threw against the wall was still sitting on the floor where it had bounced off the wall.

Three days? How is that possible?

He got off the ground and stumbled over to the hole in the wall. He looked out at the bright blue sky.

That's not the sky...It can't be. Unless...unless he's lying to me. Is it possible it's only been three days? Of course it is. I have no idea how long I've been in here. And if that's the case, that's not the real sky. It's just... just some projection of the sky that they've sped up.

Marshall slid down to the cold floor. He reached for the metallic sheet and covered himself up. His mind tumbled over the past few months. He thought about Eric, and the antique shop. He thought about Marlene and Coretta. He thought about all the ways in which his world had been completely upended in such a short time.

He thought about his parents. All those years without their memories. All those years of being utterly alone, not just without friends or family, but without even the memory of them.

I was just starting to find my place. Just starting to feel...connection. And now I'm alone again. In this cell. By myself. I've always been alone. And now I'm going to die alone.

His throat felt like he had drunk something scalding hot. He felt thirsty and at the same time wanted nothing to do with water.

Marshall crawled over to the standard ration meal on the floor and opened it. He pulled out the plastic cup of water, opened it, and drank it in one gulp. He then picked up the cube of protein and put it in his mouth. Upon the first bite there was a pain against his cheek. There was something sharp in the cube!

Marshall immediately knew what it was. *If I spit it out, they'll see it.*

He put his hand to his mouth and pretended to cough, spitting the razor into his hand. Then he clenched it softly in his fist. He crawled back over to the metallic sheet and covered himself up with it.

In that moment, he knew in the depth of his soul that Marlene had survived. He knew that she had escaped.

Marlene, she didn't forget me. She didn't leave me in here to be tortured to death.

He took several deep breaths and carefully, under the metallic sheet, put the edge of the razor against the vein in his wrist. The image of Eric, Marlene, and Charlotte slipped into his mind, followed by his mother and father.

I'm not alone, he thought and smiled, as he felt the bite of the razor cut through his skin.